AUTUMN SECRETS

Written by

Cecelia Hopkins-Drewer

ISBN: 978-0-6481160-5-9
Published by CGH Literacy Institute
Adelaide, South Australia, 2018

ISBN: 978-0-6481160-5-9

American Spelling has been adopted to match the setting.

Cover background photograph by Allan Schultz

Fictional disclaimer:
All characters and events in this work are fictional, and the story was
written for entertainment purposes. The characters have no existence
outside the imagination of the author and any similarity to persons or
events outside the text is the result of coincidence.

CONTENTS

From *The Raven* by Edgar Allan Poe

Foreword: When One Door Closes

From *The Raven* by Edgar Allan Poe

"Once upon a midnight dreary, while I pondered, weak and weary,
    Over many a quaint and curious volume of forgotten lore—
    While I nodded, nearly napping, suddenly there came a tapping,
    As of someone gently rapping, rapping at my chamber door.
    'Tis some visitor,' I muttered, 'tapping at my chamber door—
        Only this and nothing more'."

Verse 1

FOREWORD: WHEN ONE DOOR CLOSES

The community of Mystic Evermore, blissfully ignorant of the momentous events that repeatedly threaten their safety, continue on with their daily activities as if nothing ever happens. Unfortunately, I discovered that as a mere mortal, I also have no place in the more significant battles. Moreover, I am not as dear to the heart of my alluring vampire ex-boyfriend, Damien Nevermore, as I had fondly imagined. Now I resent being carried along like a piece of driftwood in the current, and long for something to change.

(Bridget Etheridge's Journal)

PARABLE SIX: THE SHADOW MONSTER

Rumors of the atrocities committed by Sven Ermore lingered in the mutterings of the town gossips. According to some, he set the town alight, perished in the fire, and then returned to haunt the innocent. According to others, he had escaped and moved interstate to run a gang of thugs. It took a while, but eventually we realized that Sven Ermore, like many villains who struck innocent women and manipulated decent men, was really 'a puny little fellow'. He had only ever been a monster because we believed him to be one.

(Bridget Etheridge's Journal)

Eduard Nevermore had invited Christopher to visit the school for the first time that day, as a sort of experiment. Christopher was a rogue vampire who had arrived with the invaders, when the Tennessee vampires had attacked Georgia. He had discovered he was unsuited to the meaningless violence and hidden until dawn. Carlice Favor, who had been among those who discovered Christopher, had taken pity on him, because he appeared to have been changed into a vampire during his late teens, just as she had been.

Christopher was kept in seclusion at Nevermore Manor for some time, while Damien Nevermore, the most powerful of the surviving vampires in Mystic Evermore, decided whether he was a spy or any other sort of threat. Damien had recently determined that Christopher had enough control of his bloodlust, and sufficient commitment to the Georgia area to join the community. The young vampire, who had some natural talent with wood-work, had accordingly been enrolled at the community college as a carpenter's apprentice.

Christopher had then been presented to Ms. Byall as a work experience candidate, sent to help with the stage and sets for the Musical Extravaganza. Ms. Byall had taken his presence at face value and set him immediately to work building a frame on which the production team would hang the backdrops. Christopher enjoyed woodwork and he was also looking forward to having friends.

The story circulated around the community was that Christopher was an exchange student. There was no real explanation as to why he was living alone in a little cottage close to Nevermore Manor instead of with a host family, but the Mystic Evermore community was used to closing its eyes to such anomalies.

When Christopher and Eduard arrived back at Nevermore Manor that evening, they found Damien surrounded with paperwork required for the management of the Blackermore Estate.

While the beautiful building and house gardens had been declared a 'national treasure', and opened to the public for recreational and educational purposes, there were a number of human staff employed to keep the place nice. The surrounding farms were also sub-contracted to share farmers, and this created a great deal of accounting.

Eduard was not interested in administration, so he passed through the common areas and retreated to his bedroom to relax for the evening, leaving his older brother with the bookkeeping. Luckily, Damien Nevermore was very good at bookkeeping. Although he appeared to be a young vampire, and officially had 'not decided' where to attend university in the eyes of the community; Damien was actually over a hundred years old and boasted several degrees from Ivy League institutions.

"Grab a bag of lambs' blood from the refrigerator if you are hungry, Christopher," Damien said casually as Christopher entered the room. "I'm trying to make a serious decision."

"What is it?" Christopher asked curiously.

"It's not your problem," Damien said. "It's just that a fair-sized bribe used to go out of the Blackermore Estate to a rather reprehensible relative of mine. This was hush money to encourage him to stay away."

"Was this relative a vampire?" Christopher inquired.

"Hybrid," Damien Nevermore replied. "One of the nastier types. And a member of the vampire aristocracy."

"Hmm," Christopher murmured. His only experience of vampire aristocracy had been Andrew Jackson, who had administered vampire affairs in Tennessee. Christopher wasn't sure that Andy Jackson was even full aristocracy, but he was highly intimidating. "Well, I'd say, keep paying this bribe."

"The thing is," Damien said. "I'm not sure my relative is even alive still. When the Mater Vampire was killed, most of the Ermore blood-line was snuffed out. Only a few of the younger vampires survived, and the Blackermores turned to stone statues."

"You could keep paying the hush-money and trace whether it was picked up by anyone," Christopher suggested. "That might give you some information."

"That is a good idea," Damien said. "Thank you Christopher! How are you enjoying the daylight ring I had Raven Booth make for you?"

"Oh it's excellent really," Christopher exclaimed. "I haven't been amongst real people during the day for years. It is rather fun - I just wish I fitted in better. I keep getting frightened I will fail."

"From all accounts you are doing well enough," Damien murmured, confirming Christopher's impression that Eduard would have called home on his mobile and filled Damien in on the day's events. Damien pushed the paper aside. "Well, that's enough. I deserve some time off before I go out to patrol tonight and continue to convince the lich community that I am big enough and scary enough to lead this area."

"I think everyone agrees that you own north-Georgia," Christopher concluded somewhat naively. Since swearing his allegiance, the younger vampire had been very loyal.

"Thank you," Damien said with a laugh. "I haven't really had any word from the South Carolina vampires about a treaty with them. Which would have been very handy. Very handy indeed."

"Why don't you just precede in good faith that the Blackermores' treaties still stand?" Christopher suggested.

"Without the Blackermores?" Damien reflected. "I would rather be sure, but that was a good thought young Christopher."

"You don't march in the shadow of a legendary general like Andrew Jackson without learning a thing or two," Christopher muttered. He had been a lowly link in the Tennessee military chain, but he had still seen how things worked.

Christopher slept in his own bed at the cottage that night. It was a luxury to be sleeping nights after so many years when he had been forced to sleep days and prowl at night. Now that he had a daylight ring, he was free to choose his own hours, tiring himself out during the day with activity like the humans did.

The next morning, however, Christopher awoke early. He donned his daylight ring and warmed a cup of lambs' blood just enough to take it off the chill, but not enough to denature its contents. Then he stepped out into the garden to watch the sun rise. He was wishing that he had someone to share it with, when Damien jumped over the back fence into the Manor grounds.

"I'm not checking upon you," Damien said diffidently, "I've just returned from patrol."

Christopher was amused. "All quiet out there?"

"Yes luckily," Damien agreed. "I don't know how much longer I can keep it up."

"You are awake day and night," Christopher reflected. "Do you ever sleep?"

"At odd hours, during the day and night," Damien said. "I begin to understand why the Blackermores did not bother with daylight rings. One waking shift in twenty-four hours is enough, and the humans were rarely a threat."

"Why don't you allow some of the others to patrol for you?" Christopher suggested.

"Werewolves have lots of energy during the days surrounding the full moon," Damien agreed. "I may let Jaylen take over then... and Jamie, the hunter, likes to let off steam occasionally."

"So you could share the burden," Christopher suggested. "What about the human Sheriff? She seems pretty keen to do her job!"

So far, Christopher had only seen Sheriff Sarah Favor in news reports on television, but he knew that the Sheriff and the Nevermores were acquainted.

"The human Sheriff doesn't exactly obey me," Damien Nevermore complained. He was as flushed as a vampire was capable of becoming, and Christopher had clearly struck a nerve. "She is also one of the reasons I patrol. I don't want her to encounter dangers she ought not to in the line of her job."

"It sounds like you care for her," Christopher reflected.

Damien laughed. "Who is the mentor and who is the adviser again?" he asked. "Come on Christopher, let us go for a walk before I go to bed for the morning."

"I would like that," Christopher said.

The young vampire longed to explore the Mystic Evermore area, but knew that Damien Nevermore was trusting him not to wander around unaccompanied at this stage. Damien set off at a loping pace, and although he had apparently been running all night, he barely appeared fatigued. Christopher reflected that after taking on the role of lead vampire, Damien Nevermore was indeed developing some characteristics of the vampire aristocracy.

Nevermore Manor was at the southern end of town, surrounded by thriving apple orchards, and yet slightly north of the area blighted by the tornado. It had beautiful grounds, which were run somewhat wild because Damien did not want to employ a full time gardener. Occasionally he relaxed by pruning the trees himself, and a contractor visited to mow the extensive lawns once a week.

At the bottom of the Manor grounds, a small stream bubbled and sang. Damien jumped into the stream bed and ducked under the wall. The stream formed a weak point in the Manor fortifications, but not many people knew about it. In times of danger, a small portcullis was lowered into the water. The bars were built from steel mixed with a very low grade of silver.

Damien waded upstream, and Christopher followed. The stream joined the river that ran along the edge of the township of Mystic Evermore, and the two vampires were able to pass by the township unnoticed. Indeed, at the speed they were running, no human eye could follow them.

They passed under a bridge at the northern edge of town, and beside the fringes where housing gave way to market gardens and working farms, and then the private wooded estates. The Woodgate Estate smelled strongly of dog to the sensitive nose of a vampire, and Christopher assumed that was where the werewolf dwelled when the moon was full. He was glad when Damien by-passed the Woodgate Estate and entered the next estate, which smelled of old magic. Vampire magic.

The Blackermore Estate felt very energizing to Christopher. There was also something else - something that told the young vampire he would be attracted back to the area on a regular basis until he had solved the mystery.

Damien halted and pointed all around.

"If you ever need a moonlit run," he announced, "That route is usually human free... and we own this land. At least - it has been in my uncle's name since the Blackermores disappeared. It is open to the public during the day... However, it should be deserted at night."

"Oh wow!" Christopher exclaimed, looking all around. "Would you really trust me out here all by myself?"

"If you stick to the river," Damien stipulated. "It used to be our secret route to visit our cousins."

Christopher nodded enthusiastically. After a couple of weeks under observation in the cellars, the land surrounding Nevermore Manor had seemed like a breath of fresh air. However, the length and breadth of the Blackermore Estate represented true freedom. Especially at night. And Christopher expected to have a few restless nights despite the daylight ring.

Damien yawned: "I'm finally tired," he admitted. "This isn't like me - sometimes I run all the way up nearby Mount Mystic."

"You have been patrolling at night for several weeks solidly," Christopher observed.

"We have to return to the Manor," Damien said. "Or I will fall asleep on my feet."

"Could I explore here a little longer?" Christopher asked eagerly. "I promise I won't get into trouble."

Damien nodded. "Take care then" he said. "Remember, some of the share farmers begin work early. And be back at the cottage by the time Eduard comes to pick you up for the Musical Extravaganza rehearsal."

Christopher nodded. In his excitement he had almost forgotten about the program designed by the Nevermores to integrate him back into human society. "I'll be back," he said.

Damien turned back into the woods and made his way in the direction of the stream, becoming a thin black blur almost indistinguishable by Christopher's sharp eyes.

Christopher turned to admire the beauties of the Blackermore Estate.

The buildings loomed dark against the brightening sky, except where a stray beam of sunlight caught the glass of a window and sparked a reflection. Early birds were chirping from the trees, and the vegetation progressed from natural to cultivated, as he walked out of the woods onto the fertile farm land. Closer to the mansion, the trees had colored leaves and appeared more ornamental, but Christopher did not plan to venture close to the house that morning.

Moreover, some of the share farmers had been fertilizing recently with blood and bone. The stale smell was not pleasant, even to his vampire nostrils, but it did tweak at his instincts, threatening to trigger the extension of his fangs. The last thing Christopher needed was to go all 'vamp' and accidentally reveal himself to a sturdy farmer with a pitchfork. So instead of venturing further onto the cultivated land, he turned and retreated into the woods, enjoying their wildness and the sanctuary they created for the native wildlife.

After a while, a glance at his wrist watch told Christopher that he ought to return to the cottage. He located the rivulet, followed it down to the main river, and out again as it branched into the stream that flowed into the grounds of Nevermore Manor. Before leaving the stream, Christopher used his fleet fingers to find and catch a fish, which he ate raw. Damien had not said that he could not catch game, and the fresh food helped sooth his craving for blood.

Then Christopher had a little time to shower and change his clothes, before Eduard's tires crunched on the gravel driveway from the Manor house to the cottage, alerting Christopher of the other boys' arrival. For some reason, both Eduard and Damien drove vintage cars. Damien had a yellow Oldsmobile and Eduard had a red Buick. The cars were nowhere as old as their vampire owners, but the Nevermores prized the retro vehicles as the one affectation they allowed themselves among the myriad efforts they made to fit into human society.

Christopher climbed into Eduard's car, pondering quietly what his one affectation might be, that would allow him to adapt back to human life. Integrating once again was something that he greatly desired, but after - he wasn't sure how many years - because there was something wrong with his memories at some stage, it was not an easy aim to achieve.

****

Classes had finished on Friday, but the students who were involved in the Mystic Evermore High Musical Extravaganza had several days of rehearsal before their gala performance on Columbus Day. The after-school practices held during term had been quite casual, allowing for sporting commitments, so Ms. Byall declared there was a lot of work to be done over the final weekend.

Generally, it was great fun to dress up and see the play come together under their very eyes. The mother's committee were providing lunch for the practices, which was another inducement. Moreover, the popular senior girls, including Carlice Favor, Anna Vaughn and Lena Lenore were playing the lead female roles.

Eduard Nevermore had been coerced into playing the romantic lead, despite the fact that he appeared a little pale and shaky after his recent bought of sickness. Nathan Vaughn and Benji Strahan had been conscripted to play the other male leads, while some of the junior girls, including Zarah Strahan, who took after her mother in being able to sing beautifully; Jeroma Tilton and Netta Davis, who both just loved an opportunity to act, were part of the chorus.

Christopher learned that Javier Tilton, (who insisted his name began with a "J"), had volunteered to accompany the Mystic Evermore High School Musical Extravaganza on the piano because he believed it would increase his popularity with the senior girls. Javier had fondly imagined himself dashing off thrilling chords, while surrounded by a doting Ms. Byall, and the girl on whom he had initially had his eye, the darkly tragic and incredibly romantic, Lena Lenore. Unfortunately for Javier, Lena Lenore had recently re-united with her former paramour, Eduard Nevermore. So Javier was doomed to patiently strike the note for them to practice sentimental love songs to each other. The look on his face whenever Ms. Byall said, "Let's take it from the top again," was almost comical to behold.

Christopher longed to make friends among the high school students, and perhaps even find a girlfriend as Eduard had. His life as a vampire had been lonely up in Tennessee, where you really had to know the right people and be a bit tougher than was his nature. Accordingly, Christopher diligently worked away on the frame Ms. Byall had requested he build. As the frame took shape, Christopher glanced at the girls who kept running in and out of the main hall. The prettiest according to Christopher's taste, was Zarah Strahan. She had black hair and beautiful brown eyes. There was something just a little bit exotic about her bone structure, Christopher's guess would be Hebraic or Mediterranean many generations back. The Star of David she wore around her neck confirmed this suspicion.

Zarah's manners were bright and she was developing an air of confidence that was unusual for a girl still in her junior year. She also had the singing voice of an angel. A little untrained perhaps, but it would develop. Christopher mentioned his interest in Zarah to Eduard one time Eduard was on a break from practice, but Eduard warned him that Zarah was semi-spoken for by Paul Booth, a young male witch who could make

Christopher's toes sizzle if he wanted.

Christopher then found himself looking at Jeroma Tilton.

The girl was lanky and going through a gangly stage, however, if she ever filled out, she would be stunning. Jeroma also had jet black hair, in her case it was dramatically paired with pink and white skin. Her lips blushed red and would be very kissable. However, Jeroma appeared to gravitate towards Benji Strahan a lot, and Christopher was learning that if he wanted to make friends and influence people, he needed to avoid already formed pairings.

Netta Davis made very bold and came up to talk to Christopher as he worked. She had a cheeky manner and bright eyes. Her light brown hair with just a hint of chestnut, was cropped shortish, and while she acted sophisticated, Christopher had the feeling Netta was very young. Moreover, Eduard whispered in his ear that Netta's older brother, Mike was very conservative and would never accept his sister going out with a vampire. In fact, Mike Davis preferred to stubbornly ignore all the signs that some of his friends were vampires.

Carlice Favor and Lena Lenore were both in relationships, so that Left Anna Vaughn. Anna was pretty in her own way, despite being school captain and having the reputation for being 'sensible'. She had long brown hair, which she wore in a practical pony tail, but which Christopher imagined would be spectacular let loose. Christopher continued working on the frame, confident that a girl who was normally responsible for organizing things around the school, would come up to inspect his handiwork eventually. He was rewarded when Anna approached, accompanied by Ms. Byall.

"You have been working hard all morning," Ms. Byall observed.

"Yeah," Christopher agreed. He was rather proud of the sturdy wooden frame. "Would you be wanting me to nail the backdrops on Ms?"

"No, I want them to be changeable," Ms. Byall said. "Each backdrop needs its own rail, please Christopher, and some hooks on the main structure to hang the rail by, please."

"Certainly Ms.," Christopher said. He tried to catch Anna's eye and smile. "Anything to help the production."

"I do appreciate your doing all this work Christopher," Ms. Byall murmured. "And just for experience too! It's a pity the programs are already printed, so I can't add a credit to you."

"That's all right Ms.," Christopher said. "I'm not looking for the credit."

Christopher hadn't really figured out what he ought to use as a surname yet. He had a vague memory of being called 'Columbus', but he had been assured among the vampire community that was not possible. The historical Christopher Columbus had been much older when he died, and vampires stay the age they were when they change, they do not experience rejuvenation. Christopher wondered whether the real Christopher Columbus had a grandson or nephew or anything, but the puzzle had never been solved. Anyway, with Columbus Day approaching, that surname wasn't going to work. The only other name that rang a bell in his mind was Arano. It was also unusual, but seemed to suit him.

Anna shyly ran a finger along the surface of the frame. Christopher knew he really ought to have warned her not to do that, because she might have got a splinter. However, he was too fascinated by the fine digit, with its neatly manicured nail and hint of clear nail polish. Apparently, Anna was not quite as 'sensible' and plain as everybody thought. Anna's finger encountered the rough edge of a nail that Christopher had broken while attempting to hammer it well into the hard wood. She gave a squeal and withdrew her finger. A bead of blood swirled on her smooth pink skin.

"You have cut yourself," Christopher gasped. "I'm so sorry!"

"It's not your fault!" Anna exclaimed.

However, she was left talking to herself because Christopher was overcome by the sight of her fresh blood. He had turned his head away and clamped his hand over his mouth in an attempt to hide the descending fangs. Anna assumed Christopher was about to vomit, and made sympathetic noises about him being faint at the sight of blood. Christopher clamped his hands tighter over his face and moaned.

"Go and get first aid please Anna," he choked.

"It's okay," Anna said. "It's nearly stopped now."

"Get antiseptic and a sticking plaster," Christopher growled through his hands. "You can never be too careful with nail punctures. Tetanus - you know."

Anna was about to explain that Tetanus was normally associated with rusty nails, when Christopher made a dash for the men's conveniences. Eduard Nevermore followed him in a hurry, as if to see what Christopher needed.

"You had better get a bandage," Ms. Byall pronounced. "Blood rule you know, to prevent infection." The blood rule was for sport, not drama where physical contact was much less likely, but Anna obeyed the teacher.

Eduard entered the male conveniences and surveyed Christopher sympathetically. "Are you all right man?"

Christopher had stuck his face down in the sink because he was worried it might have been one of the human boys entering the room. "No," he replied mournfully from its depths. "I don't think I can live among humans. I don't know how you do it!"

"It took me years, believe me," Eduard replied. "I made my share of kills before that." Eduard did not like to admit such things. He liked to be viewed as the 'good' Nevermore brother. However, in order to help Christopher, he would make an exception.

"That girl's finger bled just the tiniest bit, and I'm like this,"
Christopher continued pessimistically.

"But you didn't bite her!" Eduard exclaimed. "You have done
wonderfully."

"Do you really think so?" Christopher righted himself and his face
emerged from the sink. "What if she had seen my teeth?"

"She didn't," Eduard counselled. "And if she had - we could have
glamoured the memory away."

"Okay," Christopher was beginning to cheer up.

"You better get back out there and finish your wood-work before they
decide you are too delicate for words," Eduard advised. "Plus I've got to get
back to my song learning." Eduard looked grim at the prospect of more
practice. His voice had once been a nice tenor, which was one reason he
had been assigned the main male singing part. However, his recent illness
had drained him, and standing around practicing for hours was now a
strain. He thought he was doing a great job of hiding it, but Lena was
beginning to sense something. And that sarcastic Javier Tilton with the
perfect natural pitch, obviously knew for sure.

There was a relaxing lunch break, during which the students enjoyed
the sandwiches and cakes supplied by the mothers. Vampires like Eduard
and Carlice could consume human food, although they looked amongst the
offerings for meat-based products such as ham and chicken. They
commonly carried their own drinks in flasks, explaining the viscous fluids
away as tomato juice or strawberry smoothies. Christopher followed their
example.

The afternoon practice proceeded without further incident.
Christopher finished the framework, and began discretely erecting it around
the back and sides of the stage. He worked as quietly as possible because
the students were clustered around the piano singing.

After practice finished, Fenton Etheridge arrived to collect his
girlfriend, Carlice Favor. He was accompanied by his sister, Bridget
Etheridge. Fenton invited a few kids to hang out around their pool. The
weather was getting cool for swimming, at least for humans, who could feel
the cold, but Fenton explained Captain Etheridge had installed a solar
heating system, so the Etheridges' pool was still tolerable. The Etheridges'
pool area was also a great space for a barbeque.

"Come along then Bridget and Carlice," Fenton said. "I can fit two
more in the car, and anyone else coming to our place will have to ride with
Javier." Zarah and Benji Strahan climbed into Fenton Etheridges car,
although Zarah was frantically texting her boyfriend Paul Booth to tell him
where she was going.

Javier Titon had his driver's license, but he did not have his own car. This afternoon, however, he had the loan of his mother's car as she had no need for it on a Saturday. His sister Jeroma jumped into the front seat, while Anna Vaughn and Netta Davis climbed into the back. Javier looked pleased that at least he had a car load of girls as a reward for his musical efforts.

Christopher had been included in the invitation, but he shook his head. He was mildly frightened of the twins' father, Captain Etheridge, who had helped Damien Nevermore coordinate the battle against the Tennessee vampires. Captain Etheridge had a silver protective suit, moreover, it was rumored that he had access to silver bullets and flame-throwers and all sorts of weapons that could injure a vampire.

"I think I will spend some time with Damien up at the Manor tonight," Christopher said. "Thank you for the kind invitation Fenton."

Damien Nevermore had become Christopher's mentor as well as his sworn leader. He was grateful to Damien for sparing his life, as he truly believed that his former general, Andrew Jackson of Tennessee, would have slaughtered the young vampire at the sight of his cowardice. Christopher noticed Bridget Etheridge's expression darken visibly at the mention of Damien Nevermore. He had heard the eighteen year old girl enjoyed a brief romance with the older vampire, and even remained fond of him after their mutual break-up. However, their relations had become less cordial, as Bridget had observed the growing affection between Damien Nevermore and Sheriff Sarah Favor.

"Lena and I are going out somewhere romantic for dinner," Eduard added diplomatically. "But I can drop you off at the Manor on the way, Christopher."

Everyone said goodbye to whoever they would not be hanging out with that evening, and the students all left the hall. Ms. Byall was left behind to fuss around, planning where everyone would stand on the stage. She also turned to check Christopher's work erecting the backdrops, and found that she was very pleased. However, there appeared to be something missing… perhaps she had forgotten to give it to the young carpenter.

Ms. Byall returned to her car and looked into the back seat. She shivered as she saw the artistic impression of a dragon resting on the upholstery. Although it was only papier mâché, and some bright students had decided the dragon ought to have eagles' wings instead of the scaled reptilian wings common in picture books, the monster was effective in triggering her imagination. The drama teacher carried the sculpture into the hall and put it down gratefully. At least it would not be flopping around in the back seat as she drove home.

****

When they arrived at the hall in the morning, Ms. Byall bustled out to meet them and give Christopher his instructions. Eduard hurried away to get into costume, because that morning was to be a full dress rehearsal.

"I am absolutely thrilled with the framework you have built for the backdrops," Ms. Byall enthused. "You are really a talented young man, Christopher. What was your surname again?"

"Arano," Christopher replied. He really did not know, but it rang a bell somewhere in his mind.

"It sounds Italian," Ms. Byall simpered. She paused for a moment, clearly lost in her thoughts of Italian opera and musicals. "Or Spanish."

"I dunno," Christopher said. "As far as I know, I am American."

"We all come from different places once," Ms. Byall gave a delighted laugh. "Except for our lovely Native Americans of course."

"What did you want Ms?" Christopher inquired. Ms. Byall appeared to be getting sidetracked something severely.

"Oh two things Christopher," Ms. Byall came back to attention. "Firstly - when you have the scenery up for the first act - would you mind leaving it there for the performance tomorrow?"

"Of course," Christopher agreed with a smile. "Easy."

"Would you be able to hang around for the performance and organize the scenery changes for us?" Ms. Byall asked. "You seem so handy..."

"Yes, Ms. Byall," Christopher replied. He was pleased to be asked. "Would that be all Ms?"

"I hadn't got to the second thing yet," Ms. Byall objected.

Christopher had counted two requests already, but perhaps he had forgotten a thing or two about teachers in the long years of being a street vampire.

"What, Ms?" Christopher asked.

"The art department made me this," Ms. Byall said. The drama teacher produced the papier mâché figure of a giant eagle crossed with a dragon from the trestle where she had placed it the previous evening. If the viewer looked closer, they noticed that the creature also had an indistinct rider wearing a black cloak and hood on its back. Perhaps someone had been channeling Tolkien when they created the figure.

"I thought if we could have this pass over the stage once or twice at intervals to create a bit of excitement," Ms. Byall continued. "Could you organize that?"

"I could hang it on a cable perhaps," Christopher said. "And draw it along. When would you want it to come out?"

"During the storm I think," Ms. Byall said. "That would be a good time for the monster to come out..."

"Alright," Christopher said. "Um - and pass by like the shark on *Jaws*?"

Ms. Byall clapped her hands. "Just like *Jaws*, but up in the air!"

Christopher took the papier mâché figure from Ms. Byall and inspected it thoughtfully. He walked around to the rear of the stage and began making some plans. Most of the students had arrived and changed into their costumes. The play was beginning to look good and the singing sounded pleasant to Christopher's untrained ears as well.

After receiving his instructions, Christopher was busy backstage all morning. He finished installing the scenery for the first act and made sure the scenery from the following acts was all securely attached to rods and ready to slot into place during the brief curtain closure. He had to climb up high on a ladder to attach the papier mâché dragon and organize a pulley system whereby it could be drawn across the stage above the performer's heads.

Christopher was so busy with the arrangements, he barely noticed when the morning practice finished. Javier had closed the piano and walked away; and most of the other students had gone to change. Ms. Byall was fussing with the ticket stand she was setting up in the entry, hence the interior of the hall was virtually deserted.

Anna Vaughn must have crept up quietly, her gentle slipper-clad tread making so little noise that his vampire hearing did not pick it up over the sound of his hammering. "Hey Christopher," Anna said, making Christopher jump.

He accidentally banged his thumb with the hammer. It hurt, but vampires healed quickly, so he merely put his hand behind him. "Hello," Christopher stammered.

"The sets are looking great," Anna murmured shyly.

"Thanks," Christopher said.

"Did you hurt yourself?" Anna asked sympathetically.

Christopher shook his head. He brought his hand out from behind his back, but by now the thumb had recovered, and even the bruising faded away. Anna took his hand and inspected it.

"Oh I thought you hit yourself," she exclaimed. "That can be very painful, and sometimes the nail even comes off."

"Sometimes you get lucky and it doesn't even bleed," Christopher replied.

"Lucky indeed," Anna agreed. "Well - I'm glad you are not hurt."

"Yeah," Christopher agreed. The vampire found himself looking at her soft neck, which was exposed where she had her hair tied back in a pony-tail. The skin looked tasty and he could almost swear he saw her jugular vein throbbing.

"I was wondering," Anna began shyly. "Well - Lena sent me to ask really - would you like to come out with Eduard, Lena and me for tea after practice today?"

"It is sweet of you to ask," Christopher began. He could see the matchmaking hand of Eduard Nevermore in this invitation.

"Please don't say no," Anna begged, and the look in her eyes was so sweet Christopher momentarily forgot he was a vampire, who more regularly bit ladies' necks, than kissed their trembling lips.

"Oh all right," Christopher agreed. "Where are you going?"

"Just to the Snack Bar," Anna explained. "And we won't be late, because Columbus Day will be such a big day tomorrow."

"I will see you after the practice then," Christopher said. "If you don't mind now - I'm a little busy."

Christopher kept his attention on his work as Anna walked away. She had smelled tasty, and the vampire was struggling to keep his fangs packed away. He was glad they were going on a group date, because he would be able to rely on Eduard's presence to keep him on the straight and narrow.

At noon, the students ate their shared lunch, but Christopher kept on working. A little experimentation had shown Christopher that it might be possible to rig the lighting, so that the papier mâché monster would throw a much larger shadow across the stage, than its body warranted. Together with the stormy sound effects, it would create quite an intense moment of fear towards the end of the play.

The afternoon practice ran smoothly. Ms. Byall had scripted a typical love story between a poor sailor and a genteel young woman. The drama teacher had cleverly worked in songs like "We sail the Ocean Blue" from *H.M.S. Pinafore* by Gilbert and Sullivan; and "Blow High, Blow low" from *Carousel* by Rogers and Hammerstein. To this she had added a couple of mournful love songs from the film *Titanic*, and of course, a huge storm. Luckily Ms. Byall had decided on a happy ending, unlike *Titanic*. This meant that the sailor boy, played by Eduard would survive the dragon and the storm, to be reunited with his lover, who was played by Lena. His on-stage side-kicks, played by Nathan and Benji, would also survive to romance the female best-friends, played by Carlice and Anna.

After practice, Anna and Lena came backstage to collect Christopher, who was just tidying up his tools and off-cuts. The young vampire had always taken pride in doing things properly, and while it was a while since he had a job, he was very proud of his efforts.

"The dragon is quite frightening when it is accompanied by the sound effects and lights," Lena announced, her eyes shining.

"I love the way you are making it look bigger than it is using the shadow," Anna pronounced.

"It is doing pretty well for a papier monster created by your school art department," Christopher concluded. He had of course, in his years as a vampire, seen things that would make these girls scream and forget all about stage monsters. Lena Lenore had a knowing look about her eyes, and being Eduard's long term girl-friend, presumably knew a thing or two about the lich community. However, Anna appeared to be a complete innocent.

"Where did you all get to?" Eduard called. He stepped off the stage into the production area. "I hope you are not stealing my girl, Christopher." It was only half a joke, because by all accounts Eduard was incredibly possessive regarding Lena Lenore.

"No," Christopher returned. "I'm a shy guy really. I need to take things very slowly..." He tried to catch Anna's eye, hoping she would get the message.

Anna got some sort of message, but possibly not the one Christopher was trying to project, because she held a hand out for Christopher to hold. Christopher took Anna's hand, marveling how soft and warm it was. He thought he could feel a pulse in her thumb and looked determinedly down at the ground, willing his fangs not to emerge. He was grateful the offending teeth appeared to have begun following his conscious intent.

The group followed Eduard to his vintage car and climbed inside. Eduard drove the sort distance to the Snack Bar and parked out the front. There was another car park out the back, but it was quite full. Being school holidays, and the evening before Columbus Day, all the community youth were out looking for something to do.

There were a few locals that Christopher had not yet met in the Snack Bar that evening. They gave him curious looks because he was new in town. The Tiltons and other youth who had met Christopher at practice, were filling the rest of the students in on his status as "work experience" at the school, and he was being slotted into society just as Damien Nevermore had hoped. Christopher turned his attention back to Anna.

"What would you like?" he asked her.

"It will be my shout," Eduard added to fill the awkward gap.

Eduard knew that Christopher did not have a means of support as yet. This would be solved when his work experience became a proper apprenticeship of course, but until now, staying at the cottage in the Manor grounds, Christopher had not needed any cash.

"Ice cream sundae and cherry soda, thank you," Anna said.

"Do they have the special strawberry smoothie here?" Christopher inquired of Eduard. Christopher had yet to learn which local businesses served the vampire friendly wines and crushed ice drinks. Some cheeky vampire, probably Damien Nevermore, in his wicked days, had glamoured several shop proprietors, so they were perfectly innocent of the fact their 'special' products contained a serve of lambs' blood.

Eduard nodded. "Two of those coming right up," he observed. "One for you and one for me!"

"I will have banana topping on my ice cream, please Eduard," Lena said.

Eduard made his way up to the cashier. Christopher followed, partly because he wanted to be helpful and carry the drinks, and partly because he did not want to be alone with the girls. He envied Eduard his ease in putting an arm around Lena Lenore, just as if she did not smell so delightfully human under all her perfumes.

"Are you having fun?" Eduard asked.

Christopher nodded. "Sort of," he agreed. "It is also hard work."

"Dating isn't easy," Eduard said. "Lena and I have had our ups and downs."

"You two were on a break when you dated Christy - weren't you?" Christopher inquired.

"Yeah," Eduard agreed. "That was a mistake!"

The young vampiress under discussion had just entered the Snack Bar with her long term admirer, Wilson Bennet. Christy was dressed in a sexy fashion which attracted all the boy's eyes, and certainly put the 'vamp' in vampire. This meant the evening was taking an awkward turn, as Lena, Eduard and Christy were still not a comfortable social combination. Eduard and Christopher carried the snacks and shakes back to their booth. Lena and Eduard ate quietly, keeping a wary eye on Christy.

"I'm going to get Lena of here," Eduard murmured.

Christy had not approached the group, but something about her overly-bright manners and resolutely turned shoulders implied there was still pent-up tension. Eduard himself looked miserable from a combination of embarrassment and guilt. The matter was no longer a relationship issue, but a moral one, because the debacle had robbed Christy of her life as a human.

"Do let us stay a little longer," Anna appealed to Christopher.

"I - err, don't have a car to drive you home," Christopher stammered.

"It's all right," Javier Tilton said from a nearby table. "You can catch a lift with us."

"Thank you," Anna said.

Eduard discretely steered Lena towards the exit, while Christopher and Anna shifted across to the next table to join Javier, who was out with his young sister Jeroma. Christopher reflected that while Javier was a curious sort of fellow, he might be worth getting to know. Something about Javier's presence made Christopher feel very comfortable, and his fangs itched less, despite being surrounded by tempting smelling humans.

"We are both support staff for the Musical Extravaganza," Javier remarked to Christopher. "So we may as well stick together."

"You play for every song," Christopher exclaimed in surprise at Javier's modesty.

Javier shrugged casually. "No one looks at the accompanist. I'm surprised my name is even on the program."

Christy Strahan had noted the exit of Lena and Eduard and was now eyeing the others with open curiosity. She said something to her companion, Wilson Booth and he shrugged.

"Hey Christopher," Christy called across several tables. Her tone was bold and seductive. "Out on the town today?"

"Hello Christy," Christopher returned politely. "Yes. How are you?"

"I'm good," Christy said licking her lips suggestively. "What about you?"

"Okay I guess," Christopher muttered. He looked embarrassed.

It was his sincere hope that Christy did not pursue the conversation further. He had met her when she had visited Tennessee, however, he knew that Mystic Evermore folk believed Christy was in rehab somewhere near Atlanta, during that period.

Anna surveyed Christopher with reproachful eyes. "You know Christy already?" she asked with concern.

"I met her recently," he muttered, trying to make the encounter sound insignificant. In fact, it was Christy, in her anger and resentment at being turned into a vampire, who had incited the Tennessee vampires to overrun Mystic Evermore, bringing Christopher to town. "Trust me, nothing happened."

"Christy is way too happy with Wilson," Javier pointed out. "And before that she was all about Eduard. You have nothing to worry about Anna."

"True," Anna murmured. She looked thoughtful. There was clearly some shared secret, and while she did not mind sensing there was something more to Christopher's acquaintance with the Nevermore brothers than she had been told; she did not like to think the secret also involved the sexy Christy Strahan.

"There is a scarecrow competition tomorrow, out at the Farmer's Market. You ought to come along and join us there," Javier suggested.

"It sounds interesting," Christopher agreed.

He reflected that the community of Mystic Evermore loved its fake monsters. First there was a papier-mâché monster in the play, and now a competition to create figures designed to scare birds away from crops. Probably because the community was so busy ignoring the real creatures among them, it took extra delight in its shadow monsters.

"Most of the kids will be there as a group," Jeroma added. "It would be a good chance for you to meet a few of the others."

"Yeah, no need to make it a date or anything," Anna agreed. She appeared to be backing off the acquaintance. It was something a less confident girl might do, when there was the suggestion that her male friend had been out with a more confident girl.

"It is good to make friends," Christopher agreed.

****

The next morning, Christopher caught a lift with Damien Nevermore to the scarecrow competition. Damien was arriving early because Sherriff Favor had deputized him for the day. It was something the Sheriff did to explain Damien's authority during times of crisis and she had apparently decided it would be more consistent if she conscripted him during festivals as well as emergencies.

So Damien arrived early at the Farmer's Market complex just north of town and helped the Sherriff put up orange flags and parking signs. He also bought Sarah Favor a bunch of flowers off an early stall holder. This was not in his job description and made the Sheriff blush. She stuck the flowers in a glass of water in the cabin of the squad car, which was parked under a shady tree.

Christopher reflected that Sheriff Favor was an attractive woman despite being the mother of eighteen year old Carlice Favor. She had bright blonde hair, which was cropped short, but not too short to be feminine. Her fitness training routine ensured that she maintained a nice figure, and her maturity meant that Damien did not have to disguise any of the elements of his checkered past from her.

Damien and the Sheriff continued their security patrol, while Christopher wandered through the Farmer's Market complex unaccompanied. He was glad that he had now gained some control of the protruding fangs, and was in far less danger of revealing himself to the human's attending the festival. Being full of a breakfast of lamb's blood also made him feel comfortably mellow.

"Ferocious aren't they?" a friendly looking farmer pounced, pointing towards the assembly of scarecrows already surrounding the picnic area. He held out a hand to Christopher. "I'm Sunny Pinkerton."

"Christopher Arano," Christopher said. "It's nice to meet you, Mr. Pinkerton."

Sunny Pinkerton looked meticulously clean, as he was dressed in neat clothes for the festival, but he smelled of earth and plant matter from long days spent in the field. Christopher decided he liked the combination; it was better than the scents and colognes most humans used to try to disguise their natural smell.

"Just Sunny, Please," Pinkerton said. "I will be judging the scarecrows in a couple of hours' time, along with Mayor Woodgate - because somehow a simple farmer is presumed not to know enough about what scares crows off a crop!"

Christopher laughed. "The big-wigs have to be involved in everything somehow," he observed. He mused that Sunny must be Ivy Pinkerton's father. "What does scare a crow, sir?"

"Well, a scarecrow is meant to mimic a person out in the field," Sunny explained. "And crows are pretty smart. After a few days, when a scarecrow doesn't move, they learn to ignore it."

"Oh wow," Christopher hadn't thought of it like that.

"Now this one," Sunny said, coming to a halt before a figure in overalls, stuffed with straw, "Would be ignored pretty quickly, despite its fine face." He stepped across to another scarecrow, one that had a raggedy shirt which would flap in the wind. "This one would appear to be moving - so while it isn't as neat - it would be more effective."

"Which one do you think would be most effective?" Christopher asked curiously.

"Well, at this stage, this one," Sunny said, coming to a halt in front of a scarecrow that was dressed in a man's old clothes, had bright ribbons flapping from its straw hat, and a selection of reflective aluminum cans and empty pie plates hanging from its arms. "The ribbons create the illusion of movement, the aluminum plates will reflect in the sun at various times of day - and the tin cans may even rattle when the wind blows. Those crows are going to have a hard job ignoring this one!"

"Do you know who made each one?" Christopher inquired.

Sunny shook his head. "No they just have numbers on them, like this." Sunny bent down and indicated a tag attached to the stick near the base of the scarecrow.

"That one is so realistic it is creepy," Christopher remarked, indicating a scarecrow near the corner of the picnic area.

"Yeah, I dunno why it is wearing a suit," Sunny remarked. "Too neat and trim by far. And it's low to the ground, it's barely raised on its stick at all."

Sunny walked across to the scarecrow in question to inspect it closer. The face was so life-like it must have been a rubber mask. The hair must also have been a real wig instead of the traditional straw or wool. The hat was a deer-stalker, which seemed way out of place.

"I've never seen a scarecrow wearing a beret cap before," Christopher said.

Sunny shrugged. "I've seen pretty much everything," he mused. "Including one wearing my mother's old rose patterned skirt once."

Christopher giggled at the thought, but his mirth died as the eyes of the realistic scarecrow appeared to settle upon him. There was something different about this scarecrow. It definitely was not a human in disguise, for Christopher could not smell the tell-tale pulse of blood. It wasn't a vampire either, as no vampire could stand out in the bright morning sun like that without a daylight ring. Perhaps it was the product of witch craft. The scarecrow opened its mouth and Christopher glimpsed a row of canine teeth. They were jagged and rotten, and glinted in the sunlight.

"There!" Christopher clutched at Sunny Pinkerton. "The scarecrow moved."

"I'm sorry boy, I think you are mistaken," Sunny returned.

Christopher mused that Sunny's human eyes had probably not been fast enough to catch the brief grimace from the creepy figure.

"I expect you are right," he agreed. "Still, it is creepy. I think I will keep away from it. I think little children should keep away from it too. Perhaps you should even put a fence around it."

Christopher left a puzzled Sunny to his inspection of the remaining scarecrow figures and hurried across the market complex to find Damien Nevermore and Sheriff Favor. The police tent was stationed next to the first aid tent, and Damien and the Sheriff were available to return lost children to their parents. They would also respond to all the minor social emergencies that arose during festival time.

The first aid tent itself was operated by Sebastian Nevermore and his pregnant wife Melissa, both of whom were ambulance officers at the Mystic Evermore hospital. Sebastian Nevermore was also known fondly as 'Uncle' by the community. He was something like a hundred years younger than the vampire brothers, Damien and Eduard, but he had adopted them as his 'nephews' for appearance's sake.

"I have to talk to you," Christopher cried, bursting into the police tent to confront Damien and the Sheriff.

"What is it Christopher?" The Sheriff sounded patient. She clearly expected many minor crises to arise that day.

"One of the scarecrows moved," Christopher exclaimed.

The Sheriff laughed. "They flap in the wind," she explained.

"No not like that," Christopher persisted. "It smiled at me... all toothy-like."

"Are you sure it wasn't clockwork or animation?" Damien asked.

"Nah - not like that," Christopher said. "It was so fast that Sunny did not see. And what would be the point of an animation that humans could not see?"

"This sounds like your field," the Sheriff said to Damien with a sigh.

"And here was me hoping that we could have a nice, normal Columbus Day."

"Okay, show me this scarecrow," Damien said. He got up reluctantly. It had been pleasant sitting alone in the tent with Sarah Favor. Now Christopher had arrived, the moment was spoiled anyway.

Christopher led Damien out of the police tent and past all the stalls of produce, across the small platform erected for the entertainment, and through the picnic ground.

"In the corner by the fence," he said pointing. There was a flurry of dark movement and Christopher found he was pointing at nothing. "It's gone now."

"Perhaps I was looking at the wrong spot," Damien Nevermore said. "But I saw nothing - even with my sharp eyes."

"One of the scarecrows is missing," Christopher insisted. "The one in the corner by the fence."

"The young man is right," Mayor Woodgate announced, coming up behind Damien and Christopher with a clipboard. Mrs. Woodgate was an attractive brunette of around middle age. She was accompanied by her elderly fiancé Noah Bumble. They were one of the cutest couples around town, and Noah's presence always seemed to calm Karen Woodgate's inherent snobbery. The major was also Jaylen Woodgate's mother.

"We had twenty scarecrows registered, and now I only count nineteen in the field," Mrs. Woodgate continued.

"The youth are bringing more," Damien said, indicating the Etheridge twins and Carlice Favor, who were carrying a late entry across the field. Bridget, Fenton and Carlice were followed by Damien's brother Eduard, along with Jamie and Lena Lenore and another fresh scarecrow. Anna Vaughn was part of the group. Christopher glanced her way wistfully, and then decided his place really was alongside Damien. At least until the mystery of the grinning scarecrow was solved.

Mrs. Woodgate consulted her clipboard. "I believe those are new entries," she said. "The committee take a quick digital photograph of each entry before they tag it."

"Could we have a look at those, please Mrs. Woodgate?" Damien asked politely.

"Sure," Mrs. Woodgate handed Damien the clipboard, and Damien proffered it to Christopher.

"Was it any of those?" he asked.

Christopher squinted against the bright sunlight and surveyed the digital photographs. "It might have been that one," he said reluctantly. "It is a very poor photograph."

"The women had a lot of trouble with the camera," Mrs. Woodgate agreed. "It wouldn't focus for some reason."

"The camera focused for the others," Christopher observed wryly.

"So it did," Mrs. Woodgate agreed. "It was like - a momentary glitch. Everything is automatized nowadays, so we took no notice."

"Do you know who entered that particular scarecrow into the competition?" Damien inquired.

"As one of the judges, I'm not given that information," Mrs. Lockwood objected. "It would be most unfair to the entrants."

"But someone would have recorded it somewhere?" Damien insisted.

"Of course," Noah Bumble agreed. He had been standing quietly listening. "One of the committee ladies - perhaps old Mrs. Pinkerton - would have the full list secreted away somewhere."

"Thank you Noah," Damien said. "Good luck with your judging, Mrs. Woodgate."

Damien and Christopher trudged over to the administration tent, which was next in line from the first aid tent, and after the police tent. Sheriff Favor saw them approaching and stepped out of her tent to hail Damien.

"All sorted?" Sheriff Favor asked.

Damien shook his head. "Now the scarecrow is missing."

"We would be a laughing stock investigating a stolen scarecrow," Sarah Favor said shaking her head. "Perhaps its creator decided to withdraw it from the competition."

"That is what we are going to find out," Damien said. "I'm inquiring at the administration tent to see who entered scarecrow number 13."

"Number 13?" Sheriff Favor scoffed. "You have to be kidding."

The Sheriff followed Damien and Christopher into the administration tent, where Old Mrs. Pinkerton was just finalizing entries for the apple pie baking competition.

"Grandmother Pinkerton," Damien began. "Could you please tell us who entered scarecrow number 13 into the competition?"

"I'm not supposed to, the competition hasn't been judged yet," Grandmother Pinkerton returned sharply.

"Please, Mrs. Pinkerton," Sheriff Favor said. "Official police business."

Grandmother Pinkerton reached into the large folder resting on the table and turned over the pages. A slight frown gathered between her eyebrows. "No," she muttered. "It is not possible. And I did not take that booking, or I would have known better."

"What is it Grandmother?" Damien asked anxiously.

"Scarecrow number 13 is registered to Sven Ermore," Grandmother Pinkerton replied. "As far as I know, he has been dead almost a hundred and fifty years, along with the other town pioneers."

Damien Nevermore and Sheriff Favor exchanged significant glances.

"Thank you Mrs. Pinkerton," Sheriff Favor said. "You have been very helpful."

"I hope it's just a harmless prank," Mrs. Pinkerton wrinkled her forehead in distress.

"I'm sure a prank has been played somewhere, and we will get to the bottom of it," Sheriff Favor assured her.

The Sheriff marched out of the administration tent and into the relative privacy of the police tent. Once the canvas had closed around them, she turned to Damien Nevermore and placed a manicured hand on his chest, giving him a small affectionate shove against the center post. It was a surprisingly assertive gesture for the normally well-mannered woman. Damien stepped backwards obediently.

"Wasn't that the person who sent someone to put a bomb in your car?" Sarah Favor hissed.

"Yeah," Damien replied gently. "But don't worry about me - I can take care of myself. Place an officer on Uncle and Melissa."

The Sheriff nodded and activated her radio. "I need extra staff at the Farmer's Market," she barked. "Immediately."

"Is this the reprehensible relative you were worried about?" Christopher inquired.

"Yes," Damien growled. His fangs were showing, and he sounded desperate despite the presence of the Sheriff.

"I can't imagine how Sven survived when the hunters killed the Mater Vampire," the Sheriff sounded puzzled. "You got sick, Eduard almost died and the Blackermores... um... err, disappeared."

"Perhaps Sven survived because he was out of the state at the time," Damien suggested. "Or perhaps it was because of the other components of his make-up. He wasn't just one of Henrietta's get."

"What do you mean?" Christopher was puzzled.

Damien sighed. "The Nevermores and our older cousins, the Blackermores, were born into the Ermore family before they were turned - of course. But Sven was thought to have been part Woodgate... the product of someone's dalliance. He certainly carried the Woodgate curse. Moreover, he is said to have had an affair with the sister of Great-Grandmother Booth - breaking her heart and stealing her witch magic."

"So the vampire side of Sven Ermore died, what would have been left?" Sheriff Favor asked.

"A mean, two hundred year old, werewolf warlock," Damien sighed. "Just slightly less powerful than vampire aristocracy."

"Well, that is one thing at least," Christopher was determined to see the bright side of things.

"He should be vulnerable to both silver and iron then," the Sheriff spoke determinedly. "I will call Captain Etheridge on duty."

"The wolf-whisperer may also be effective," Damien mused. "Contact Javier Tilton."

"The trouble is, we don't know where Sven went when he left here," Christopher observed. "Assuming that he was masquerading as scarecrow number 13."

"It sounds like something that would amuse Sven," Damien said. "And the Woodgate Estate adjoins here. I think it is a fairly safe guess that he has retreated through the Woodgate land to the Blackermore Estate."

"We need to keep everyone safe, but I don't want to have to disrupt the festival," the Sheriff declared determinedly.

"I think you will be fine, if you increase security," Damien observed. "Sven was always... strategic.

"What do you think he wants?" the Sheriff asked sharply.

"Sven may well believe this territory ought to be his," Damien said. "As he is the oldest of the surviving descendants."

"So - the matter is between you and him then?" Sheriff Favor inquired.

"Basically yes," Damien Nevermore said. "But Sarah, remember, Sven is not above using pawns. And it could be anyone I am perceived to care about. Starting with Melissa and Uncle, but even including you and Bridget."

"Now that you protect the entire Mystic Evermore area, it could be absolutely anyone," Christopher pointed out logically.

Damien frowned. "I hope Sven hasn't degenerated that far," he declared. "That would make him entirely too unpredictable."

****

The Sheriff's reinforcements began to arrive, and Sarah Favor gave her orders efficiently. Another undesirable character had been observed loitering around town, she announced. This character was a lunatic who might be under the impression that he was one of the town founders who had died about a hundred and fifty years ago. He might also believe he could perform magic tricks and turn into a wolf.

The officers were to surround the festival area and protect all the attendees, especially Melissa Nevermore, who was vulnerable because she was pregnant, and the bevy of school children attending the carnival. If the officers saw the stranger, however, they were not to approach him unless they were carrying their special issue pistols with the silver bullets, and armed with a pair of iron hand-cuffs.

At the completion of the festival, the officers were to transfer their protective attentions to the Mystic Evermore High Musical Extravaganza, which would be the next major assembly point for community folk. Like a terrorist, this mad-man was expected to strike some time when the people were all assembled.

Christopher reflected that it was rather admirable the way the Sheriff had her officers trained to fight and respond to a paranormal threat. The men did not need to believe in vampires or werewolves, they just needed appropriate strategies and a plausible explanation.

Meanwhile, Damien Nevermore pulled out his mobile phone and began organizing his own troops. He texted his brother Eduard and asked him to keep the high school students together as much as possible, and guard his ex-girlfriend Bridget Etheridge at all times. Eduard replied with concern, asking what was wrong.

Damien replied: "Not sure - Sven?"

Eduard's typing appeared shaky as he texted in reply: "Our sire?"

"We don't know," Damien replied. "Take all precautions just on case."

To tell the truth, Damien and Eduard had never been quite sure whose blood they had in their system that fateful day. Elisha claimed that he had given the younger Ermore cousins his blood out of love. Later the same afternoon, Sven had appeared and claimed he had been the one to turn Darrion and Edvard, motivated purely out of spite.

The young Ermores would surely have perished if they had remained human, and they sincerely hoped the act had been done out of love. Being turned into vampires was a shock that traumatized both brothers for the next twenty years. When they gained some semblance of control, Darrion and Edvard had changed their surname to 'Nevermore', and then returned home to offer their allegiance to Elisha.

Elisha, who had changed his surname to 'Blackermore', had accepted their allegiance. He deliberately kept the Nevermore brothers and Sven as far apart as possible. The reality was, if both older vampires were correct in claiming they had given the young Ermores blood that day, they would have dual sires. This was a complication that no one wanted to confront.

The hereditary hunter Jamie Lenore was Damien's most physically powerful ally, so he asked the youth to keep an eye upon Sebastian and Melissa. Jamie acquiesced, although he did return the complaint that if there was hunting to do, he would rather be doing it.

Damien: replied "Maybe later".

After that, Damien called Javier and Jaylen to the police tent to brief them himself. Jaylen was extremely powerful in his wolf form, however, being a Woodgate, could make Jaylen a target for Sven Ermore's schemes. Damien therefore suggested that Jaylen stick close to Eduard and the other school seniors. Jaylen nodded happily, excepting during the full moon, he was happy to be in the middle of a group, and wanted to keep his girlfriend, Ivy Pinkerton, by his side.

Finally, Damien turned to Javier Tilton, the wolf whisperer, who was his most potent psychological weapon. Javier listened to Damien's story gravely, and then shook his head at the request to make himself available to confront Sven Ermore, as soon as the mad-man could be located.

"It's not possible," Javier said soberly. "I have promised to play for the Musical Extravaganza, so I will be on the piano all afternoon."

Damien looked disappointed. "We made a good team before," he said.

Javier nodded. "In this case, though," the wolf whisperer said thoughtfully, "You face a direct competition between yourself and your ancestor, regarding who owns the area. I think that my subduing him might actually send the wrong message."

"So what should I do?" Damien cried.

Javier looked thoughtful. "I haven't tried this before," the wolf whisperer said, "But I may try to enhance your natural charisma. If you believe that you are more powerful, you might just become so in reality."

"It's worth a try," Damien agreed glumly.

Outside the police tent they could hear shouts of excitement. The scarecrow competition had been judged and the crowd was moving on to the apple pie table. Christopher reflected that he was missing a lot of everyday fun, something he had been looking forward to after obtaining his day-ring. However, events in the tent were pretty intense too.

"I also think that you need the witches," Javier suggested. "If you are dealing with a two-hundred year old warlock."

Damien frowned. "Raven Booth is still mad at me for sending Jamie out to fight against the Tennessee vampires."

Javier laughed. "Raven knows that Jamie loves to hunt," he said. "And I think you might find she is pretty angry with Sven Ermore, if as you say, he stole powers from her Great-Aunt."

"Okay," Damien agreed.

The vampire sent a text to Raven inquiring whether it was possible she could craft a spell to strip the stolen powers from Sven Ermore. Raven replied in the affirmative, providing they could get close enough to touch the warlock for the final stage. Especially as the stolen powers were Booth powers, it was likely that herself, John or Paul could call them back, and even become a vessel to hold the powers permanently.

Then Javier sat Damien down on a chair in the police tent, and placed him under a form of hypnosis, affirming the vampire's natural charisma and glamour. Like he said, the wolf whisperer had never attempted this strategy before, but the power of suggestion was a wonderful thing. If Damien really believed that he had dominance over Sven, he might be able to exert it.

Javier stepped back from Damien and looked at his watch. "I have to get some lunch at one of the stalls, and then move onto the hall for the Musical Extravaganza," the wolf whisperer observed. "The Sheriff announced the community ought to travel in convoy as much as possible."

"Well thank you for your assistance," Damien said. "I should be able to manage now." To tell the truth the vampire was reeling from the rush of his newly found confidence.

"Be careful," Javier warned. "Don't get drunk on your own vanity and make a mistake."

"I will try," Damien responded wryly. Luckily, vanity was more Eduard Nevermore's failing than his brother Damien's. Damien had always been more prone to self-loathing.

Christopher followed Javier Tilton and Jaylen Woodgate out of the police tent. He too had a commitment to the Musical Extravaganza that afternoon. He did not really need lunch, but he figured that if he could find some special wine or strawberry shake on one of the stalls, it would fortify him for the afternoon to come. Lunch eaten, the High School students travelled in convoy across to the hall, where Ms. Byall was busy with the final details for the Musical Extravaganza. The drama teacher looked surprised to see Christopher.

"Oh Mr. Arano," Ms. Byall exclaimed, "I thought you were already here. There have been a couple of noises from the back of the stage."

"It wasn't me," Christopher exclaimed and hurried around to inspect the sets.

Nothing seemed to be out of place and there was no one to be seen backstage.

"It must have been my imagination," Ms. Byall exclaimed. "I could have sworn there was someone back there."

"When you are alone in a place like this Ms.," Christopher advised. "It is safest to lock yourself inside."

Mike Davis and a few of the boys who were not involved in the play had been conscripted to help set out the seats. They settled to with a will, and the hall was almost ready when the parents and other members of the community began to arrive. Soon the hall was full and the curtains creaked open to reveal Javier Tilton playing the piano.

Javier had originally only volunteered to accompany the Musical Extravaganza to be around the girls. However, as Ms. Byall observed the musical talent placed at her disposal, she had become more ambitious and he was now delivering a thundering concerto to introduce the action. Then the lovers, Eduard and Lena appeared on stage to begin their courtship.

They sung a touching duet and subsequently were joined by the other couples involved in the play. A couple of group songs were sung, and the lead characters frolicked, while the chorus sang several lively tunes. The lovers were eventually separated as Eduard's character went out to sea. The curtains closed and opened again to reveal a dismal scene as Lena's character was led to believe that Eduard might never return. The heroine fell down in a faint, and the curtains were closed again.

In the next scene, the velvet fabric opened to show Eduard's character, supposedly on a boat during a great storm. Javier played dramatic crashing chords on the piano, and Christopher worked the ropes he had attached to the papier mâché dragon to pull it across the stage. The carpenter cleverly dimmed the stage lights, and backlit the dragon to create a menacing shadow.

The audience gasped. The excitement created by special effects was greater than they had expected, and Eduard's character literally cowered under the shadow of the approaching dragon. Javier's tune changed as the dragon passed overhead. Then, Christopher turned the normal stage lighting on again, and Eduard began to sing a wistful song of home and love. Soon his ship was presumed to be approaching the shore, where he climbed out and stood on a strip of dry land.

The curtains closed and opened again, to reveal a scene set in the heroine's home. The hero arrived to revive her wilting frame and the final tunes became happy and frolicsome again. The audience, who loved a happy ending, sighed with satisfaction; then they went mad clapping and cheering!

This year, with Javier Tilton's highly trained fingers on the piano, the production had reached a whole new level. Ms. Byall had also been free to concentrate on training the performers and directing the play, producing a much more convincing drama. The cast were called forward for several bows, and Javier was entreated to play a short encore piece. As the hoots and cat calls continued, Ms. Byall signaled to Christopher to make the dragon pass over the stage once again.

Christopher was eager to please, and began to haul on the rope that pulled the dragon along. This time, something was wrong. There was a lot of extra resistance. Christopher kept tugging, assuming the rope had just caught in something or jumped its track on the pulley. The dragon slowly wobbled into view, with a figure clinging to the rope above it. The figure was a small, untidy man in a dark suit.

The man, who was presumably Sven Ermore, let go the rope and leapt across the stage, capturing Anna Vaughn in a clumsy embrace and holding her in front of him like a shield. The hybrid and Anna stood on stage in front of the audience in a terrifying tableau, while the Sheriff's men and Captain Etheridge looked to their leader to make sure this was not part

29

of the act.

Anna screamed horribly and the spell was broken. With the weight off the dragon, the papier mâché dragon careered toward Christopher at top speed. It came to the end of the pulley, and jerked off the rope, striking Christopher on the head.

If he had been human, Christopher would have been knocked out. As it was, he was momentarily confused and did not see where the man went. Both the man and the maiden, had disappeared. The audience were left gasping, and the county police officers circled around advising people to stay in their seats. A panic and rush towards the door was the last thing the community needed just then.

A letter fluttered to the ground. Lena Lenore tentatively picked it up and noticed that the envelope was addressed to the town of Mystic Evermore. It was doubtless a ransom demand. Lena handed the letter to Sheriff Sarah Favor, who had marched up onto the stage accompanied by Damien Nevermore.

"Give it to me," Damien demanded anxiously and intensely. He forgot to say 'please', and the Sheriff's eyes narrowed angrily.

"You know we don't negotiate with criminals, Damien," the Sheriff snapped. "He has kidnapped one of my citizens, so this is my jurisdiction!" She tore the letter open and skimmed its contents while the crowd waited in suspense.

Damien fidgeted impatiently as he remembered Javier's warning not to become over-confident and make a deadly error. Offending his long-term ally the Sheriff might be just such an error.

"The mad-man wants us to acknowledge him as town leader or he will hurt Anna," Sheriff Favor reported. "This is totally unacceptable."

"Whoever he is, he is truly a lunatic," Mayor Woodgate stammered, coming forward onto the stage. She looked pale and shaken. "Everyone knows that I am the elected town leader."

"In cases like this, my dear," Noah Bumble pronounced placing a protective arm around Mrs. Woodgate, "It is the Sheriff to whom we look to defend your leadership."

"Ah of course, if it is a matter of law enforcement, then Sheriff Favor might be considered the leader," Mayor Woodgate admitted. "The powers of the Agrarian Council are primarily in governance and administration."

"Whilst I am merely a humble servant sworn to uphold your defense," Damien Nevermore observed more diplomatically than before, and with a touch of his vampiric charisma in evidence. "I want the chance to help. Give me the letter please, Sheriff."

Sheriff Favor relented and handed the letter over to Damien Nevermore. He read it through seriously, noting the more personal nature of the message. Of course, Sven was play-acting, but if the human residents were to acknowledge Sven Ermore's authority, Damien would have difficulty continuing to manage the paranormal community.

"We must rescue the young girl at once," Damien declared.

"I agree," Sheriff Favor announced. "But we do not know where he has taken her."

"I believe the letter contains a clue," Damien said.

"It is merely a description of some building that stood some one hundred and fifty years ago," the Sheriff sounded puzzled. "The town has changed since then."

"When I was a boy, there was a spot much like he describes, on the Blackermore Estate," Damien Nevermore declared. "If you could perhaps order the fire service to see everyone home Sheriff, Captain Etheridge and I will lead an elite team to rescue Anna."

"Good thinking," Sheriff Favor declared. Damien had cleverly given her the impression that she was in charge. "You and Captain Etheridge will lead an elite team Damien. What else?"

"The civilians need organizing," Damien said. "You could take Anna's mother and brother back to your house and comfort them until more is known about the situation."

The Sheriff nodded. "Of course!"

Damien added just a little dollop of persuasion to his tone to help the Sheriff believe this was her all own idea. "There are also school students to take care of.... Fenton and Bridget will be alone if Captain Etheridge is with me."

"Excellent," the Sheriff observed. "Fenton, Bridget, Mrs. Vaughn, you can all come along with me."

"A threat has been made against the town leader, so Mrs. Woodgate and Jaylen need protection," Damien continued. "You might want to set up somewhere defensible. If your house is not large enough - you are welcome to use Nevermore Manor."

"I think my house will do quite well," the Sheriff declared spiritedly. "I generally take precautions in my line of work - and it is only against one man."

"One man that we know of," Damien intoned cautiously. "And a mad-man at that."

The Sheriff turned to Ben Vaughn and asked him to activate the Fire Brigade to help ensure the hall was evacuated safely. Ben was worried about his niece Anna, but he was a good man in a crisis and he agreed that the town well-being came first.

****

The members of the Fire Brigade who had been on duty helped the people leave the hall in an orderly fashion; while the Sheriff's men patrolled the roads to make sure all community members reached home safely. Mystic Evermore citizens were well educated about the need to lock their doors and stay inside during times of crisis.

Sheriff Favor invited Ben's distressed sister Daria, who was Anna's mother, back to her house to await the outcome of the rescue effort. The Sheriff also invited Fenton and Bridget Etheridge, together with Jaylen Woodgate and his mother Karen, to spend the night at her house as well.

Mayor Lockwood followed the Sheriff home obediently. She was shaking like a leaf, and Jaylen, whose first impulse had been to protect his girlfriend Ivy Pinkerton, quickly saw the wisdom in accompanying his mother. With so many vulnerable people in the house, the Sheriff decided to keep a squad of her most trusted officers on hand as well.

Christopher tugged at Damien's shoulder. "I want to be on the elite team that goes to rescue Anna," he whispered.

"Of course," Damien agreed. "I will be grateful for your assistance."

Christy Strahan approached Damien. "Count me in too!" she cried.

"But you hate the Nevermores," Christopher exclaimed in surprise.

Christy shrugged. "I hate Eduard," she said. "Damien always tried to help me… besides, I am bored trying to be a good girl. If there is any chance of a fight, I would like to be in it." The young vampiress flexed tautly coiled muscled arms in anticipation.

"You are welcome to help too Christy," Damien agreed. "Now where is Wilson?"

"Here!" Christy's boyfriend, Wilson Booth called.

"Wilson, your cousin Raven is preparing a spell for me," Damien said. "Get your father John, and brother Paul, and ask Raven to meet me in the grounds of Blackermore Estate as soon as possible."

"Sure Damien," Wilson replied. "Whereabouts on Blackermore Estate?"

"There is an old cottage," Damien said. "It is run down now, and home to the birds. But it still has running water - over on the north side of the Estate."

Wilson Booth nodded. He was apprenticed to the local plumber, Robbie Strahan and hence knew every tap, drain and sewer in Mystic Evermore and surrounds. Even those attached to run-down cottages and abandoned farms.

Captain Etheridge had made a brief trip back home and his Jeep full of equipment was parked just outside the performance hall. Damien, Christopher and Christy piled into the vehicle. At the last minute, Javier Tilton decided to jump into the back seat beside Christy. The vampires would probably have made better time on foot, but Javier and the army captain would not have been able to keep up. Even though he was only human, Captain Etheridge was a fearless fighter and his protective equipment rendered him resistant to attack.

"Drive please," Damien urged.

"Anna must be terrified," Christopher exclaimed.

"She is going to be impressed by your rushing after her like a knight in shining armor," Christy teased.

"It's not about that," Christopher mumbled.

"I know," Christy said. "Anna's not the first girl you notice when you walk into a room, but she is a good friend nevertheless."

"Something like that," Christopher muttered. He didn't really know how he felt, dating a human girl had its pitfalls. However, he did feel responsible, because the bad guy had dropped down off the pulley rope that Christopher had installed.

Captain Etheridge's jeep ate up the road through the north of the village, across the bridge, past the Farmer's Market and alongside the Woodgate Estate. They also passed the Old Mill Farm and Pinkerton house. Then they turned onto the Blackermore Estate. Damien gave the Captain directions, so that he passed the mansion and area open to the public and continued down a dirt track towards the northern fringe of the estate.

Finally, the party pulled up at a dilapidated stone cottage in the shadow of Mount Mystic. The ruin was covered with climbing rose bushes, and would have been quite beautiful under any other circumstances. However, evening was falling, and the black bulk of Mount Mystic loomed ominously. The broken door of the cottage gaped jaggedly and the interior was dim. Damien and Christopher leaped out of the jeep and approached the cottage door. Christy followed and began to circle around to block off the back entrance. Captain Etheridge turned to Javier. He held out a finely meshed chain mail tunic.

"You might need some protective gear too boy," the Captain offered.

"Oh thanks," Javier said. He picked up the loose fitting tunic and slipped it over his signature black coat without bothering to disrobe. Luckily the large arm holes were very accommodating. "I don't normally bother about that sort of thing."

"I know you have your magic voice," Captain Etheridge said, "But you never can be too careful."

"Yeah - I haven't tried the voice against a warlock," Javier admitted.

"I don't think it would work on a normal witch," the Captain said. He picked up a rifle. "Luckily, Sven is half-werewolf." He loaded the gun. "Silver bullets."

"Just don't hit Damien, Christy or Christopher," Javier joked.

The Captain took up a position sheltered by the remnants of a rock wall, and trained the sights of his rifle on the cottage. He had a cool laser sight for night shooting. Javier also ducked behind the broken stone wall.

"Sven Ermore, are you here?" Damien called smoothly.

"Ah little cousin," Sven replied. "You were quicker than I expected."

"I remember this place well," Damien returned.

"It seems no one else does," Sven chortled.

"I'm coming inside to get the girl," Damien said. "She is not part of this. Please let her go Sven!"

"I wouldn't do that, little cousin," Sven Ermore warned. "Feel what I got from the witches."

A small fire-ball whizzed past Damien's cheek. It singed his face as it passed. Damien winced. Fire could kill a vampire.

"Always the pyromaniac, Sven," Damien retorted. "You must have been disappointed that the bomb you placed in my car did not kill me earlier this year."

"On the contrary," Sven replied. "I would have been sorry to lose you. I could use a servant or two from the Ermore bloodline."

"Neither Eduard or I are interested in serving you, Sven," Damien was firm.

"As I am your sire, you have little choice," Sven began, but Damien stopped him.

"Elisha gave us his blood that day," Damien responded clearly. "I don't know whether we had any blood from you - but I deny a sire bond."

"It's not something you can deny," Sven sounded confident.

"I deny it," Damien repeated. "Elisha Ermore was my sire."

Damien and Sven appeared to be at a stalemate in the battle of wills when Raven arrived with John and Paul Booth. They had followed Wilson's instruction to meet on the Blackermore Estate, and after they arrived at the mansion, Raven sensed the use of magic on the northern fringe.

"I see you cannot face me alone little cousin," Sven jeered. "You need to bring witches along."

"Quite reasonably as I don't have magic," Damien agreed.

"We aren't just any witches," Raven declared. "We are Booth witches and we have come to claim what is our own."

Raven began an incantation, and Paul snuck up to the cottage.

Peering through the glassless window, while Sven was occupied with Damien, Paul Booth was able to cast the thread of a dream catcher towards the warlock. Sven brushed the dream catcher off his back, but a thread caught in an inaccessible place. Sven howled and tried to reach in-between his shoulder blades.

Raven continued to chant:

"Powers of the Booths ever new,
stolen away without care due,
come back to your owners true,
and settle in the body prepared for you," she cried.

John Booth reached out and felt for the powers. This was the risky part, as John Booth had been drained of all but a trickle of his natural powers when he had attempted to bind the Mater Vampire, Henrietta Ermore in his youth. He had been a relatively unpracticed witch, and while he had won that round, performing a binding that lasted many years, he had also done irreparable harm to himself.

The gamble that the Booths were taking was that while John had lost his powers that time, he had retained the capacity for power. If his capacity had not been burned out, he might be able to received Sven's stolen power. Raven continued to chant and John continued to reach out.

Sven gave a howl of horror as the Booth powers he had once stolen began to leach out of him and float towards John Booth. Raven was a powerful young witch, and there was no casting Sven could make strong enough to cancel her spell. The powers entered John Booth, and he collapsed with a howl as they burned their way through him.

Paul ran to his father's side and bent over him.

"Dad," Paul cried. "Oh Raven, we talked about this - the risk was too great."

"Give him a moment," Damien said, laying a restraining hand on Paul's shoulder. "He may take control of the power yet."

John Booth writhed in agony and then slowly began to calm down. He opened his eyes and looked at his son. Then he closed them and fainted with a final shudder. Paul rubbed his father's hands and implored him to return to consciousness.

"Please, please wake up Dad," Paul cried. "You were the best Dad ever. We didn't care that we were poor, you were always there for us. You always knew what to say and what to do to fix everything."

"That is nice to hear," John Booth murmured from behind closed eyelids.

"Oh Dad - are you going to be okay?" Paul cried.

"Give me a little while," John said. "That fellow had stolen a great deal of power it seems, and this body hasn't held power for many years."

Paul and Raven gently lifted John between them, and began to support him towards the station wagon. John had been the driver on the way over, but it was probably Raven who would drive back to town. They opened the passenger side door and the exhausted male witch slumped into the front seat.

Sven Ermore suddenly burst out of the cottage and began to grapple with Damien and Christopher. He morphed half-way towards werewolf form and tried to bite at them. Damien and Christopher struggled to restrain the wolf head and stay away from the gnashing teeth as werewolf bites were poisonous for vampires.

Javier Tilton rose from his crouching position behind the brick wall and used his wolf-whisperer voice to command Sven to return to his human form. Captain Etheridge struggled with his rifle sight to get a clear shot at Sven, and not hit Damien or Christopher. Finally, he let off a bullet, winging but not killing the hybrid.

Sven gave a howl and wrenched himself away from Damien and Christopher. He disappeared into the woods and they heard crashing going in the direction of Mount Mystic.

"Let him go," Damien said reluctantly. He was holding his hand and his fingers were dripping blood.

"Did he get you?" Captain Etheridge exclaimed in alarm.

"Just a scratch," Damien said. "Poisonous, painful and paralyzing, but not deadly."

"Here let me have a look," the Captain laid his rifle down in the jeep, and pulled out a first aid kit.

Christopher took the opportunity to enter the cottage. He gave a cry of alarm at seeing the interior was empty. "Anna is not here!"

"Over here," Christy said, appearing around the side of the cottage supporting her friend. "I took the opportunity to sneak her out while the men were fighting."

"That was terrifying," Anna sobbed. "Thank you all so much for coming after me."

"Get in the Jeep girls," Damien ordered. "Captain Etheridge, thank you for bandaging my hand. Christopher, it looks like you and I are riding on the roof."

"You can travel with us in the wagon," Raven Booth offered.

"I would like to go with Anna," Christopher announced. "Javier - would you mind swapping?"

"Sure bud," Javier Tilton said amiably. He shrugged the protective tunic off and handed it back to Captain Etheridge. "Thank you for the loan Captain. I'll see you tomorrow."

"Are you sure you don't want to continue pursing Sven tonight Damien?" Raven inquired.

"I can't," Damien said. "I'm bitten. I need to recover. Sven is shot and he has lost his warlock powers. He has been vastly weakened and I be able to face him down later."

"Fair enough," Raven said. "John could do with the recuperation time too."

The Booth witches climbed into their car, along with Javier and Damien. The drove off towards the village, and Christopher climbed into Captain Etheridge's jeep next to Christy and Anna. Anna appeared to have fallen asleep from trauma and exhaustion. Christopher glanced at the girl's pale face. She seemed far too young and vulnerable to have been a kidnap victim.

Anna sighed and moved against Christy's shoulder, which she had been using as a pillow, completely unaware of the fact that her former friend had become a vampire. Anna also did not know that the young man she was hoping to make her boyfriend was a vampire. Christopher felt a flush of guilt. He was not ready to tell Anna what he was, and neither was he ready to commit to the close contact required for an intimate relationship.

"I'm glad she is safe," he murmured.

"Yeah," Christy breathed.

"But I don't think I can do it..." Christopher continued. He did not try to explain further, but Christy was following his line of thought.

"Well," Christy murmured. "For me and Wilson - it works. But for me and Eduard, it didn't. If you are not sure - don't hurt her."

"Good advice," Christopher agreed.

Captain Etheridge drove to Sheriff Favor's house, where they proudly united Anna with her tearful mother. Daria thanked them effusively and then left for her own home, with her daughter Anna, and friend Christy Strahan at her side.

Captain Etheridge then collected Fenton and Bridget and returned to his own home for the rest of the night. He dropped Christopher off at Nevermore Manor on his way home, although this required him to take a circuitous route.

Christopher found that Damien Nevermore had arrived home, but was weak with fever from the bitten hand. He decided to spend the night at the Manor house instead of his small cottage. Just in case Damien's condition worsened or there was anything he could do to help his mentor.

****

Christopher was awakened early the next morning by a thunderous knocking at the Manor door. Eduard appeared to have spent the night at Lena Lenore's place, and Damien was sleeping the poison off, so it was left to Christopher to answer the door. He did so rubbing the sleep out of his eyes.

The caller was an angry looking Sheriff Favor. She was clad in her uniform and looked as though she had barely slept the night before.

"I have to know," Sarah Favor demanded. "Did Damien glamour me last night? After everyone else had been picked up, I ended up guarding Karen Woodgate, while my deputies guarded me! Jaylen Woodgate was at my place too, but I'm not sure whether he was guarding or being guarded."

"I wouldn't know for sure," Christopher said. "But I do know that Damien isn't up to a lot this morning."

Sarah Favor looked concerned. "Whatever is wrong?" she asked.

"Werewolf bite," Christopher said. "Has a nasty effect that lasts a few hours. I'm sure he will be up and about later."

"Did you get Sven?" Sheriff Favor asked.

"The Booth witches stripped Sven of his warlock powers, and Captain Etheridge lodged a silver bullet in his arm," Christopher reported. "But he escaped onto the slopes of Mount Mystic."

"So he is only a third the threat he once was," the Sheriff mused.

"Yes, except that he thinks he has some sort of seniority over Damien, he is beginning to look less menacing," Christopher agreed. "Like the scarecrow once the crows get to know him. Or my papier mâché monster without the lighting effects."

The Sheriff laughed. "I'm not sure what you mean by that - but it sounds good," she said. "However, I think I will hang around until Damien is better, if that is all right with you."

"Of course," Christopher said. "I'm sure Damien will want your... err... advice."

Damien stirred sleepily about an hour later. "Sarah what are you doing here?" he murmured sleepily.

"I was angry because I thought you glamoured me," Sheriff Favor replied. "Now I find you are injured! Seriously, Damien, we both know that Karen Woodgate is not the town leader that Sven Ermore is targeting."

"To be honest, I was concerned more about Jaylen," Damien murmured. "Because of Sven and the Woodgate curse."

"Why didn't you just say?" Sheriff Favor demanded.

"I don't know - confused," Damien muttered. "I had people I cared for on all sides. Sebastian and Melissa - my remaining human family, my ex-girlfriends and vulnerable people around town. Too many fronts to fight. I needed you to hold one for me."

"Poor Damien, finally learned to care," Sheriff Favor scoffed.

"I have cared for a long time, Sarah," Damien murmured. "It's just no one believes me."

"And this poison?" Sheriff Favor picked up Damien's bandaged hand and the vampire winced.

"Almost worked out of my system," Damien said.

"If you go out again, I want to go with you," Sarah Favor declared.

"Perhaps," Damien murmured weakly. "We will see where you are needed most."

Sarah Favor leaned forward, intending to give Damien a kiss on the cheek, but Damien reached for her with weak arms, and pulled her mouth towards his. Their kiss lasted a long moment, and then the Sheriff pulled away.

"Not this again Damien," Sarah Favor murmured.

"It is not anything 'again'," Damien objected. "The first time you did not know what I was... and I admit I was looking for connections in town. It was a false start. If we got back together now - it would be honest."

"I'm not ready," Sarah Favor murmured.

"It's not me, it's you," Damien joked. He was growing stronger by the moment. "I'm getting out of bed in a second Sarah, and I don't believe I am wearing pajamas."

"I am not a little girl, Damien," Sarah Favor objected, but she blushed pink and backed out of the room. The front door slammed shut behind the Sheriff, as she went on her official way once again.

Damien pushed back the covers and swung his feet to the ground. He was actually wearing boxer shorts! Christopher laughed. It might have been wrong of him to eaves-drop on Damien's conversation with the Sheriff, but he was fascinated. Theirs was a mature, true love that Christopher longed to find. The Sheriff may not have agreed to a relationship today, but Christopher had little doubt that she would eventually admit how much she cared for Damien Nevermore.

"It's not a peep-show Christopher," Damien called out knowingly, and Christopher appeared from the adjoining room door.

"Yes sir," he said.

"I need lamb's blood," Damien requested. "I would like bacon and eggs, along with a stack of pancakes, but they wouldn't do my system any good. Fetch me a blood bag from the refrigerator please."

Christopher obediently fetched Damien the lamb's blood and then stood over his mentor as he drank.

"May I suggest sir," Christopher ventured. "That you would recover quicker with something fresher?"

"The Sheriff wasn't willing," Damien growled. "And I never take without permission nowadays."

"What about the young girl - Bridget?" Christopher suggested. "I know she looked angry with you - but underneath that, I think she cared."

"I am not going to take advantage again there, either," Damien said. "And yet, perhaps you are right. Run down to the hospital and see whether you can get a transfusion bag without being detected."

"Alright," Christopher was glad to be on an errand out of the house.

Damien had instructed Christopher to 'run', but Christopher judged that a brisk walk would be more discrete. He also stopped to discretely gather a few wild-flowers from the river bank as he passed. It would help to make him look like a legitimate visitor at the hospital.

Christopher was still learning his way around town, but the way to the hospital was clearly signed, and also when he began the approach, the smell of human blood was strong. Christopher tucked his fangs securely away in his jaw and marched straight in through the front door.

The young vampire was surprised to see Anna Vaughn sitting in the waiting area.

"Hey Christopher," Anna cried. "It is real nice of you to come and see me."

"I wasn't aware you were sick," Christopher stammered in confusion.

"Mum thought I ought to be checked over after my experience," Anna continued. She turned to her mother. "Mum - you remember Christopher - he helped rescue me."

Christopher nodded shyly to Anna's mother: "Good morning Ms. Vaughn."

"Are these flowers for me?" Anna cried, laying claim to the bunch of wildflowers. "You are so sweet."

"Yeah," Christopher let the bunch of flowers go to Anna, and stood waiting awkwardly. "I say Anna - there is something I need to talk to you about."

"You don't want a girlfriend," Anna said. "I wasn't completely asleep last night when you were talking to Christy, you know. I got the meaning."

"I'm sorry," Christopher said.

"Don't be," Anna replied. "You are right to be cautious. It seems I am always cautious." A small tear escaped the corner of her eye and slid down her cheek.

"I'm sure there is someone for you somewhere," Christopher assured her.

Anna shook her head. "Not amongst this crowd," she murmured.

"Perhaps when you go away to college?" Christopher suggested. "You look like the type to have applied to the best colleges."

"You are right," Anna said. "That means only nine more lonely months of high school."

"You have friends," Christopher said. "And I - haven't found the right person yet either. I'm not dropping you for anyone else!"

"At least that is some comfort," Anna sighed.

Christopher remembered his errand for Damien, and the fact that it was rather urgent. "I have to go now," he said. "Please take care."

"Oh I will," Anna said. "I have no intention of being kidnapped ever again."

Christopher had learned to sneak in his years as a vampire. He pretended to leave the hospital to satisfy Anna's perceptions, and then entered through a side door. He found himself in a service area, where a lot of laundry was waiting to be washed. There were a couple of generic white coats amongst the laundry, and Christopher debated briefly whether it would be better to be dressed as a member of the staff.

As Christopher was attempting to access the medical storage, which wouldn't be open to visitors, he decided to don a white coat. He sincerely hoped that technicians wore these coats as well as doctors, because he did not think he could pull off pretending to be a doctor. There was a map on the wall. It was designed to educate staff on emergency evacuation procedures, but luckily had the blood bank area marked clearly.

Christopher set off at a brisk walk with his head discretely bent down as if he was deep in thought. Luckily he passed no one. It was still early and staff were busy assisting patients with bathing, dressing and breakfast.

Christopher reached the target area, and opened the laboratory door. Luckily the room was deserted. He grabbed a couple of bags from the refrigerator. Spying a handy cooler box, he decided to pack the blood bags in ice and carry them discretely in the container. He heard voices outside in the corridor, and ducked down behind the bench in case someone was approaching the room.

The voices became fainter as the staff proceeded with their duties in other areas. However, Christopher did not dare linger in the laboratory. Slipping discretely out of the door, he walked swiftly along the corridor and exited into the laundry area. Christopher pulled his white coat off, and placed it back on the washing pile, then he ducked out of the door.

Christopher did not dare pass the main entrance carrying the medical cooler box, so he blended into the shrubberies. The rear of the hospital gardens bordered on the river, and Christopher remembered Damien had taught him the channel formed a sheltered corridor around the outskirts of the township.

Christopher thought he heard the drone of a lawn mower, presumably operated by some punctual gardener. He leaped off the river bank, landing dexterously in the water, which came about to his ankles at this point. The trailing leaves of the weeping-willows that lined the river bank closed over his head. He was safe from detection.

Christopher normally had a good sense of direction, but he must have taken the wrong turn amongst the rivulets that morning, because he eventually found himself in an area he recognized, since it was the border of the Blackermore Estate. By rights, Christopher ought to have avoided the Blackermore Estate, because Sven Ermore had last been seen escaping its northern border. However, something seemed to be calling out to him. It felt like the remnants of the old vampire magic that he had sensed on his first visit to the estate.

Christopher climbed out of the river and set off in the direction of the Blackermore Mansion. He halted in the front garden to admire the beautiful water fountain. Two statues were positioned so that they gazed pensively into the water near the fountain. One statue depicted a fine featured, formally clad man. The other statue featured a beautiful woman of indeterminate age.

Christopher presumed that the statues depicted Damien's elder cousins, the Blackermores. The carved figures sort of fitted the description, although, Christopher could not understand why their heads were hidden by such wide brimmed hats. Surely, an artist would want to carve a portrait of the person and not just the clothing.

The woman was wearing a veil which hung down from her hat and partly shrouded her face. Christopher stepped closer and angled his head so that he could gaze into the woman's face. It was stunningly beautiful. Damien and Eduard were both handsome men in their own way, but their cousin Rachel had been gorgeous.

Christopher fell to his knees before the statue and gazed up in wonder. He reached out for the hem of Rachel Blackermore's dress and his fingers touched cold stone. Rachel Blackermore had been one generation removed from vampire aristocracy. An unknown vampire from another state ought not to be touching her in real life, but Christopher found himself overcome with longing. He felt that the statue of Rachel Blackermore depicted a woman Christopher could have dedicated his heart to loving. Even if she had barely responded to him.

A sound startled Christopher and he looked up. Eduard Nevermore was eyeing him with amusement. The other vampire was accompanied by Javier Tilton and Jaylen Woodgate. Jaylen was panting, and slightly wild eyed, as if he had recently transformed back into as boy from his wolf form.

"Come - I've got the car to take you back to the Manor," Eduard said.

"I've obtained the blood," Christopher announced, indicating the cooler box. "I just got rattled and confused leaving the hospital."

"Well let's get going then," Eduard sounded impatient. "Damien is waiting."

"Where were you all night?" Christopher asked Eduard curiously as he climbed into the car.

"Well I saw Lena home safely and guarded her for a few hours," Eduard said. "Then I received word from Captain Etheridge that Damien was injured - so I went out again to patrol, as he couldn't."

"Jaylen tracked you from the hospital this morning," Javier explained. "It was a risk to allow him to go wolf with Sven around, but we were counting on the injury Captain Etheridge gave Sven last night placing him under some sort of disadvantage."

"You were in the water at first, but you were on the edge for most of the route," Jaylen observed. "You left a trail. Visible only to me of course."

"Interesting," Christopher mused. It was something to say, because he wasn't really interested.

"What were you doing - worshiping my cousin?" Eduard asked, while keeping his eyes on the road.

"Rachel was very beautiful," Christopher said. "I don't think I am cut out for dating human girls like you do. I want someone like her."

"You know we think that is not just a statue of Rachel," Javier informed him.

Christopher was surprised. "Not a statue?"

"We think the real Rachel and Elisha were turned to stone when the Mater Vampire was destroyed," Jaylen explained.

"Perhaps Damien could wake her for you," Javier mused with a wistful tone in his voice. "That would be incredibly romantic." Javier was a great fan of anything gothic or mysterious, including frustrated and impossible love affairs.

"If Damien could wake Rachel or Elisha he surely would!" Eduard observed. "It would help solve his problems with Sven, and the rest of the country!"

"I know what you are saying must be true," Christopher agreed, but a wild secret hope had sprung up inside him. He vowed that he would find a way to bring Rachel back to life, even if he had to devote eternity to the project. And surely, if he was able to revive the vampiress through love, she would be so grateful that she would love him back.

Eduard pulled the car up in the driveway in front of Nevermore Manor. "Well here we are," he said. "Go inside and give the blood to Damien, it will do him a world of good."

****

They arrived back at Nevermore Manor and Christopher gave the blood to Damien, who accepted and drank with a little embarrassment. The effect was immediate, with all traces of the bilious color and feverish temperature caused by the werewolf bite fading immediately. A few more minutes and Damien would be as food as new.

"I'm curious about something," Christopher said as they were waiting for Damien's complete recovery. "What did you guys do during the war?"

Eduard shrugged. "Which war?" he inquired.

"I was a child during the American Civil War," Damien frowned. "I don't remember a lot."

"Then again," Eduard added, "We were turned just before the First Boer War...but we had other things on our minds."

"World Wars One and Two," Christopher said.

"I wasn't even born," Javier exclaimed.

"Me neither," Jaylen agreed.

Damien looked serious. "I travelled to Europe to enlist during the First World War," he said. "I saw some of the worst of the fighting, and then was captured. I became a prisoner of war. I eventually escaped and after that, I had to lie low for the duration."

"I was a spy," Eduard said. "Something to do with my being brilliant with languages."

"Most of the time, I didn't know where Eduard was, or which side he was on," Damien laughed.

"The sign of a good agent," Eduard said. "But that is another story...what about yourself Chris?"

Christopher looked vaguely uncomfortable in the face of so much valor. "During the Spanish- American War, I honestly didn't know where my loyalties ought to lie," he said. "Being partly Spanish myself. By World War I & II, I had resolved that. I joined the Home Guard, because I didn't want to leave America."

"A valid and worthy choice," Damien observed.

"Do you guys always get involved in human conflicts?" Javier asked curiously.

Damien shook his head. "No, sometimes we have our own priorities," he admitted. "Now we can't afford to wait too long before getting after Sven. He would be healing almost as quickly as I am."

"A silver bullet is poison to a werewolf," Eduard explained for Javier's benefit. "But it's not fatal unless it's lodged in his heart or his brain."

"Still, the Captain did well to wing Sven," Damien said. "It gave us a breather."

"Are we taking Captain Etheridge with us today?" Christopher inquired, curious as to the extent of cooperation with the human army captain.

Damien shook his head. "No, Sebastian and Melissa insisted on going to work as usual, so the Captain will be riding in their ambulance to protect them. He is the only human that would stand a chance against Sven unaided."

"What about Jamie Lenore?" Javier enquired. "Wasn't he guarding your relatives?"

There was a light crunching sound on the gravel, as Jamie bypassed the gateway and leapt lightly down off the stone wall. He had a massive crossbow strapped to his back, and a quiver of silver tipped arrows at his side. Knowing Jamie Lenore, as the hereditary vampire hunter, he likely had a concealed blade or two on his person.

"What about me then?" Jamie inquired. "I got stuck on guard duty last night and missed all the fun."

"We hunt today," Damien said calmly. "I always promised you would be in on it!"

"And everyone's girlfriends?" Christopher asked, reflecting Damien had been keen to have Bridget Etheridge guarded the night before.

"It being school holidays and all, Bridget, Ivy, Carlice and some of the juniors have decided to hang out at our house with Raven and Lena," Jamie announced. "They are having a girl's video afternoon, and I'm pretty sure Sven won't want to face an angry witch once again. Especially now that he has lost his Booth powers."

The sound of wheels on the driveway alerted the group to the arrival of the Sheriff and her two most trusted deputies. The Sheriff climbed out of the jeep and surveyed the assembly with an air of authority. Sarah Favor appeared to under the impression that she was in command. "Are you nearly ready Damien?" she called.

"I also promised the Sheriff she would be part of the team, but I made sure she brought along her own guard," Damien said with a grin. "Well armed with pistols and silver bullets too!"

"That's one way of doing it," Christopher agreed.

At a nod from Damien, Jamie Lenore climbed into the back of the Sheriff's Jeep alongside one of her deputies. The two vampires, Javier and Jaylen climbed into the Oldsmobile alongside Damien. The Sheriff sniffed with disapproval at Damien's prize vintage car, and then backed her jeep out of the driveway. She turned the vehicle in the direction of Mystic Evermore town center, then crossed the bridge, passed the Farmer's Market, and the market gardens.

The Oldsmobile followed, until they passed the private estates and pulled up in the car park on the lower slopes of Mount Mystic recreation park. Jamie and the deputies climbed out of the jeep, and stood waiting.

Damien parked the Oldsmobile, and Christopher climbed out of the front seat. Eduard, Jaylen and Javier climbed out of the back.

The Sheriff turned to Damien: "I've always dreaded leading a man hunt on the slopes of Mount Mystic without Elisha Blackermore's assistance," Sheriff Favor admitted.

"I'm here to help," Damien confirmed, assuring.

"I am grateful," the Sheriff said, and her deputies nodded.

Javier retreated into some shrubbery to help Jaylen transform into his wolf-shape. Jaylen would be able to cover the ground much quicker as a wolf, and might even sniff out his fellow werewolf. He would be accompanied by Jamie Lenore, whose supernatural strength and speed would barely slow him down. When the change had been effected, Damien sent Javier to join the Sheriff and her deputies in searching the main recreational areas.

"Why don't you take the main path Sheriff?" Damien suggested. "Be very thorough with the greenhouses and anything the madman could have used as shelter overnight."

The Sheriff and her deputies nodded in assent. "Good idea!" While none of the humans were cowards, they did not relish searching the steep slopes on the wild side of the mountain. The park lands and paths created for the pleasure of visitors to the mountain, represented fairly easy and safe passage for the human party. They could also be of the best service covering this area. However, Damien fully expected to discover Sven hidden on the rougher slopes. The lead vampire turned to his fellow vampires, Jamie Lenore and the wolf with a vicious glint in his eye.

"Fancy a cross country run?" Damien asked.

The others nodded enthusiastically.

The three vampires, the werewolf and the hunter spread out across the wild slopes of Mount Mystic in the shape of a fan. Christopher found that running was a pleasure, and covered his territory in happy leaps. He did not know exactly what he would do if he found Sven, but it was good to exercise his supernatural strength and skills unhindered.

As he ran, Christopher noticed the magnificent eastern white pine trees, interspersed with red cedar. Jasmine and mountain laurel plants grew in gaps, and several varieties of hairstreak butterfly flitted about in sunny patches. He could hear a number of bird calls, but was unable to determine whether they were from different species, or the mockingbirds that inhabited that region.

It did not take long for Christopher to circle the mountain several times and come to the conclusion that their quarry was not within his fifth of the area. Occasionally his passage frightened a white tailed-deer into flight, but the wildlife in general appeared undisturbed.

A high pitched whistle from Jamie Lenore called Christopher in another direction. The whistle was of too short a frequency to reach normal human ears, but the super-sensitive hearing of the wolf and the vampires perceived the sound. Christopher turned and ran towards the noise. He found that Jamie Lenore holding Sven Ermore immobile at arrow-point. Jaylen was still in his wolf form, and was guarding the enemy werewolf from the opposite direction.

The ground was littered with the mangled bodies of woodchucks that had been preparing to hibernate during the winter. Sven must have nosed out a nest to eat, in order to assist his recovery from the bullet injury. A few big brown bats had been pulled out of their roosts in the trees during the night, and their broken bodies lay strewn on the ground. Moreover, the feathers of a few doves and other birds showed they had been caught and been consumed light bones and all.

Christopher shivered at the sight of the small animal carnage, although he supposed he ought to be grateful the werewolf had not had access to a nourishing farm animal from the estates. It was also fortunate he had not mustered the strength to hunt the larger forest animals, like bobcats. Another thing Christopher noticed, was that Sven Ermore was much shorter than he had seemed the previous evening, and Jamie Lenore actually towered over him.

Christopher could feel the thud of powerful feet on the ground, and the noise told him that the other vampires were coming. Eduard and Damien pulled into view and Sven snarled at the sight of his rival. The enemy may not have been well enough to hunt large animals the previous evening, but now he was clearly able to posture.

"Damien Nevermore," Sven growled. "You lived to crawl after me did you?"

"It takes more than a werewolf bite to knock me down," Damien replied.

"And yet - you do not dare to follow me alone?" Sven taunted.

"I rather like the team approach," Damien replied with civil amusement.

"Oh - so do I!" Sven agreed. "How sure are you of your team members' loyalty?"

"Sure enough to chance it," Damien returned.

Sven concentrated upon Eduard. "Young cousin," he growled. "Why don't you come over here?"

Eduard attempted to remain behind Damien, but to his consternation, he could not resist the former hybrid's glamour. Sven Ermore was no longer a vampire, but he had either retained a few of his vampire powers, or inherited similar powers from his werewolf-side. Eduard found himself compelled to step between Sven Ermore and Jamie Lenore's silver arrow.

Sven laughed. "You stand to lose a brother Damien," he said.

"Tell Jamie to shoot anyway," Eduard begged. "I couldn't stand becoming Sven's pawn."

Jamie lowered the arrow. "I won't let you use me Sven," he declared. "I refuse to execute either Nevermore brother."

"Still - you are a hereditary vampire hunter..." Sven mused. "I ought only to have to enhance your natural inclinations." The former hybrid turned his attention to Jamie Lenore, but after a few moments, he did have to admit defeat. A hereditary hunter could not be compelled. Obviously Jamie cooperated with Damien Nevermore through choice and common interests, not any form of coercion.

"Interesting," Sven said. "But the wolf is mine."

Jaylen yelped in alarm as the older werewolf turned his attention towards him. Sven projected waves of fear, and to his own great humiliation, Jaylen found himself lowering his head and forepaws to the ground in submission. "Noooo," the wolf howled on the wind in horror at being turned against his own allies. He clenched his teeth tightly to stop himself from snapping at anyone.

"I won't have you humiliating my friends," Christopher said, stepping between Sven and the cowering Jaylen.

Sven turned his attention to Christopher, and the younger vampire felt the powerful probing of the older mind. However, it was not the mind of his sire, or indeed anyone along his bloodline, so Christopher was able to stand firm. Sven looked surprised and probed further.

"A vampire not of the Ermore line," the enemy mused. "How interesting. Why would you support Damien Nevermore?"

"Because the vampires of this area took pity on me and offered me a new life," Christopher said. "And Damien is becoming a fast friend."

"Two for me and two for you," Sven remarked to Damien. "What an interesting equation. Assuming you can continue to resist me yourself Damien?"

"Oh believe me, I can," Damien declared staunchly. "Before I became leader of this area - I might not have been able to. Even last night - I hesitated. However, there are too many people I love, and far too much at stake for me to consider giving in to any weakness."

"Humans?" Sven snarled. "Poor creatures that weaken and that die after seventy years on this planet? I may have lost my immortality, but even as a werewolf, I look forward to an extended existence on the earth."

"They will be miserable years if you cannot love," Damien declared.

"Love is a human folly," Sven cried.

"I don't believe that," Damien declared. "It gives us the power to see beyond ourselves and take action for the greater good. Our willingness to be vulnerable occasionally is also our greatest strength, in that it brings us the cooperation of others, without resort to violence and intimidation."

Sven laughed in scorn. "My strength is that I only care for myself," he declared. "It has kept me safe, and given me power over others for more years than you have been on this planet. You looked ridiculous, trying to defend all the different parties that you loved - but like that model monster in the town hall, I was able to throw a frightening shadow far bigger than my actual form across the landscape."

"You lived with a false sense of security," Damien observed. "Based on threatening women, horrifying the community, and keeping your superiors in fear of acting directly against you."

Damien drew his sword out of the sheath at his side. He stepped up to Sven and prepared to thrust it through the enemy's heart. According to Captain Etheridge's rules, which the community had abided by of late, because the captain was working on a 'cure' for vampirism, all creatures that could be restored to their humanity deserved a second chance. However Sven was too degenerate and scorned the very humanity that Captain Etheridge would strive to restore.

Sven choked in alarm. "You don't dare do that," he cried. "What if killing me causes you and your brother to die as well?"

"That is a risk I am willing to take to be free of you," Damien cried. "Do you agree Eduard?"

"For sure," Eduard replied stoutly, although he was physically still compelled to hold the position Sven had maneuvered him into.

"We grew up frightened of you," Damien said. "Our mother shuddered as she spoke your name and our father promised he would protect her from you. As I grew older, I learned that many women in the community feared you...because no one knew exactly what had happened to your first wife!"

Sven laughed. "In the end," he gloated, "Your father could not protect your mother from me. I sneaked back one afternoon and raped your mother while your father was out working."

Eduard gave a cry of horror, but Damien remained stony faced. "I have always suspected as much," he said, with the wisdom of the elder brother.

"Then I arranged the 'accident' which took your parent's lives," Sven continued. "I really meant to kill you boys too..."

"So why didn't you?" Damien demanded sternly. "Instead of turning us? I have always wanted to know."

"I had injured you severely," Sven admitted, "But that cursed Elisha interfered. He fought me to a standstill even though you were mortally injured."

"It all ends now," Damien cried. "No more women will shudder in fear, and no more small children will be frightened that Sven Ermore will be coming to get them. No men will be forced to do your bidding either in your crime syndicate."

Sven lunged towards Damien with his lupine claws extended. Damien drew his elbows back towards himself, and then thrust the sword forward in a compact action. He pierced Sven through the heart without scratching Eduard, whom Sven was using as a shield, or Christopher, who had stepped forward to protect Jaylen. Sven clutched at the sword in amazement.

"I didn't believe you would do it," the former hybrid cried. Damien and Eduard both braced themselves for the shock of the killing of their sire to go through their bodies. They had both survived the death of Henrietta Ermore, but this could still be fatal. Moments passed, but nothing happened.

"Tell us who our true sire was," Eduard demanded. "It has driven me mad for years not knowing..."

"Elisha gave you his blood," Sven admitted. "The best I could do after that was claim to have given you my blood earlier and become your sire. Then Elisha was so scared of harming you that he dared not dispose of me." Sven slumped to the ground and his life blood pumped away.

Damien gave orders for Jamie and Christopher to carry the body back to the Blackermore Estate, and laid in the vault with his name on it. It was a pity that Sven would be buried near Damien and Eduard's parents, but over a hundred and fifty years had elapsed since their death, so their corpses were unlikely to be disturbed by the newcomer.

The party had just about reached the boundary between the slopes of Mount Mystic and the Blackermore Estate, when they encountered Sarah Favor and her deputies. Javier, who was a wolf-whisperer, had sensed the disturbance through his connection with Jaylen. Knowing that something was wrong, his expression had betrayed his concern to the Sheriff. Sarah Favor had insisted that they turn around and march the other way, even if the terrain was wild.

The Sheriff inspected the body carefully. "What happened Damien?" she demanded.

"He resisted arrest," Damien replied grimly.

"I take it that is the truth?" Sarah Favor asked searchingly. "You didn't just decide it was too awkward to place him under arrest to await trial for his current crimes?"

"His current crimes are mild compared to his past crimes," Damien explained. "And you would have had difficulty prosecuting him for them."

"I appreciate that Damien," the Sherriff observed. "However, whenever I deputize you - I expect you to operate according to the law."

"Sven did resist arrest," Jamie Lenore added his voice as witness. "He was violent and dangerous and had to be subdued."

"Where are you taking him?" one of the Deputies asked curiously.

"To the cemetery on the Blackermore Estate," Jamie admitted.

"Won't that add credence to his mad claim to have been Sven Ermore?" the Deputy asked puzzled.

"It may," Eduard said. "But it seems he might have been some distant relative after all - so we don't know where else to bury the body."

"The Sheriff could organize something," the other Deputy suggested. "A grave for a John Doe perhaps."

"No," Sheriff Favor mused thoughtfully. "The coroner will have to inspect him of course. And certify him dead. But if he was a relative of the Blackermore's - a descendant with a similar name say - Damien had best put him in the family plot."

****

It was some days later that Christopher was seated beside the fountain in the garden of the Blackermore Estate. He had taken to visiting the Blackermore Estate daily, and sitting for hours in front of the statue of Rachel Blackermore. This was possible because the fall holidays and the brief community college break had coincided, and Christopher was not due to resume his apprenticeship until the next week.

He heard a sound behind him and turned to see Anna Vaughn approaching. She was accompanied by her young friend Netta Davis and Nettas' older brother Mike Davis. They had apparently all been out riding on their bicycles. Christopher was slightly surprised to see Anna, but not unduly disturbed. After all, the Blackermore Estate had been opened to the public for educational and heritage purposes.

"Hey Christopher," Anna said, hailing him from some distance. "Someone told me you had been spending a lot of time here."

"It's true," Christopher admitted. "It's so peaceful."

Anna jumped off her bike and leaned it against the side of the old stone mansion. It would not do any harm there. Netta and Mike Davis dismounted and did likewise.

"Do you mind if we join you?" Anna asked.

"Of course not," Christopher said. There was not much else he could say. His daily communion with the stone statue was intensely personal, but also unexplainable.

Anna slid down beside him on the stone step. Mike and Netta sat down as well. They chatted casually about school stuff for a few moments, and then Anna turned back to Christopher.

"Did you enjoy your work experience?" she asked.

"Ah - yes I did," Christopher responded, somewhat surprised to be able to answer truthfully.

"I believe Ms. Byall was very impressed," Anna said. "She just forgot to thank you because of all the excitement - you know."

Mike was gazing at the statue of Rachel, and Christopher felt an illogical surge of jealousy. No one else must develop the sort of intense admiration he had for the statue.

"The statue is very beautiful," Mike observed in the manner of a boy who has recently discovered the delights of female companionship.

"Yes, it is," Christopher admitted. "Is it very like her?"

"If you mean Rachel Blackermore," Mike observed, "I never met her. But the grandmothers say it is a very good likeness."

"Let us ride our bikes down to the stream," the restless Netta cried, and Anna rose to follow her.

"Goodbye Christopher," Anna cried. "I'll be seeing you around."

"Sure Anna," Christopher agreed. "Have a good afternoon."

Mike remained seated beside Christopher and both boys gazed at the statue of Rachel Blackermore. The statue continued to gaze at the fountain, and modestly sheltered its face underneath the stone veil that extended from the stone hat.

"Funny thing," Mike said. "There were no reports of a statue being here before the Blackermore's disappeared."

"Funny coincidence," Christopher mused.

"Of course, it's very possible the statues were erected just before the end," Mike observed. "However that came about."

"Of course," Christopher agreed wryly. He had heard another theory, but Mike was not the sort of boy to be interested in such things.

"I wouldn't be sitting here too long though," Mike added. "It would be too easy to imagine the statue was winking at you. And I'm not the imaginative type. Not imaginative at all!"

Mike stood up and collected his bike from against the wall. He planned to go after Netta and Anna, on their ride through the rest of the Blackermore Estate.

"Are you coming?" Mike asked, inviting Christopher along for the bike ride. "There is nothing else to do in the school holidays around here."

"No, I'll just sit here for a while," Christopher said. "And then I am due back at Nevermore Manor."

"Have fun," Mike said.

"I will," Christopher said.

Christopher sat still. He was consumed with the idea that the prosaic Mike Davis had somehow seen the statue of Rachel wink at him. "Did you wink?" he whispered.

The statue did nothing. It remained impenetrably beautiful.

Christopher waited until Mike Davis had ridden away on his bicycle, and then engaged the statue in his earnest gaze once again, but it would not wink at him. He stood up and touched the hand of the statue, where it clutched the basket. As far as Christopher could tell, the hand was cold and stone like. However, a drop of moisture had congealed just below the eye and began to roll down the statue's face.

"Don't cry," Christopher whispered. "I will find a way of freeing you from the stone. I swear."

Christopher was suddenly surrounded by heavy drops of autumn rain that soaked through his jacket, into his shirt and trousers. The sky was covered with dark clouds and he could hear the squeal of the girls and Mike as they abandoned their bikes and sought the shelter of a building. Perhaps it had just been another coincidence that the first drop had rolled down the statue's face. However, Christopher felt he was bound by his promise to someday free the woman he hoped to love from her encasement in stone.

****

PARABLE SEVEN: SOMEONE TO LOVE ME

"It all started with the puppy that insisted on following Javier Tilton around. I probably would not have talked much to Javier otherwise, as I considered him something of a poser - going around clad in a long black coat with his face painted white like a vampire. My first boyfriend had been a real vampire and I was not fooled by Javier's Goth act."

(Bridget Etheridge's Journal)

Bridget Etheridge had treasured her feelings for Damien Nevermore for some months after their official break-up. The vampire youth had advised Bridget to find someone who could offer her marriage and children, but Bridget had been unable to feel any sense of urgency. After all, Damien and she were still good friends, and he had been such a support when her mother died. However, the night of the war with the Tennessee vampires, Damien had made special arrangements for the protection of his former and more mature girlfriend, Sheriff Sarah Favor, which made Bridget feel rather foolish for hanging on to her sentimental attachment to their relationship.

After coming to the realization that her relationship with Damien Nevermore was truly over; Bridget looked around for a source of solace, and settled upon the idea of volunteering for the local pet shelter. This activity had the advantages of giving her work experience, as well as earning credit points for community service for her senior year. It also put her into daily contact with small furry creatures, and created an unlimited supply of cute cuddles.

It was fun to clean the display cages, serve the healthy animals with food and water and pet them to make them suitable for adoption by a family. Most adoptions were good ones. The shelter made the prospective owners sign an agreement that they would provide the pet with food and housing, love and veterinary attention, as required for the duration of its natural life. A few owners were frowned upon, it was well known in the community that they adopted too many animals, and neglected some or all of their pets.

There was one woman, Mrs. Grey who was known to spoil her dogs, while she neglected her cats severely. Several cats and even a dog, had been returned to the shelter when the woman tired of them, others were known to have died from accident and general lack of protection. The Sheriff had been alerted, but no charges had been laid, as it was not a crime to adopt too many pets, at least in a country town like Mystic Evermore.

It had been a good Saturday morning so far, Bridget had cleaned all the cat cages and petted two kittens who were so fluffy and cute she knew they would find homes quickly. They were males too, which always helped. Families liked male cats because their operations were slightly cheaper and they could be released for a lower price. Bridget had privately named these cats Tiger and Tomson, because both were tabbies.

Eduard Nevermore, who was Damien's brother and a senior in Bridget's class at Mystic Evermore High, had also come to work at the animal shelter as a volunteer. Eduard was quietly doing penance for accidentally turning his former girl-friend Christy Strahan into a vampire like himself, but most people did not know that. The community, and even Christy's parents, remembered the incident as merely a local accident.

At first, the animals had been unsettled around Eduard, perhaps sensing his cold blood and in-human nature. However, he had learned to speak soothingly, to them and could soon tame a wild kitten or noisy puppy in minutes. Strangely, the birds were still jittery around Eduard, but then not everybody had to work with the birds.

Bridget looked up and was horrified to see the dog-lady, as she privately called her, had entered the animal shelter. It was only a few minutes to closing time, and Bridget had hoped that the animals were safe from the woman's clutches for another week. However, Mrs. Grey greeted the staff member at the desk cheerfully.

"Are there any new animals?" Mrs. Grey cried.

"I'm really busy just now," Jenny Lenore, who managed the shelter said, rustling through the record book. She pointed Mrs. Grey in the direction of the cat cages. "Bridget should be able to help you."

Mrs. Grey approached the cat cages. "Hello Bridget," she called.

"Hello Mrs. Grey," Bridget replied politely as she was obliged.

"Are there any new cats?" Mrs. Grey asked.

"It's almost closing time," Bridget said, glancing ostentatiously at her watch. "I don't think I have time to show you around now." She pointed Mrs. Grey in the direction of the dog cages. "I think Eduard might have a new dog or two to show you."

It wasn't hard to distract Mrs. Grey from the cats by mentioning the dogs, as she vastly preferred the dogs anyway. The middle-aged woman swiveled and went over to the dog cages, calling for Eduard. If she found a likely dog and chose to adopt it, the canine would likely get better treatment than a cat would at her hands.

"You have escaped my lovelies," Bridget said to Tomson and Tiger as she locked the cages so no more visitors could enter. "If you are lucky, a nice family will be through early next week and you will go to loving owners."

Eduard had interested Mrs. Grey in a Jack Russell terrier, and the woman headed towards the adoption desk with the animal in tow. Eduard locked the dog cages behind the visitor, and came to stand beside Bridget.

"I sometimes wonder whether that woman has something strange about her," Bridget whispered.

Eduard shook his head: "Nothing that I can sense," he said. "She is just extremely selfish and perhaps a little unhappy."

"Do you think the dog will be alright?" Bridget asked.

"I hope so," Eduard said. "She seemed to genuinely like him. When she only has two dogs she is okay, it's when she has three or more that some become nuisances and get returned to us in a sorry state."

Eduard said, "Goodbye," to Bridget as he was meeting his girl-friend Lena Lenore at the Snack Bar for lunch. Bridget was just about to leave, when the woman at the reception desk called her over.

"I'm sorry Bridget," Jenny Lenore called. "I know you have finished your time, but I wondered whether you could take one of the dogs from around the back for a walk?"

"I guess I can, Jenny," Bridget agreed, although she was not looking forward to going around the back to collect the animal in question. Bridget had learned that animal rescue had its sad side. Of the hundreds of animals that came into the shelter, a good percentage had to be put down. Some were too diseased to be kept alive, some simply too old, some too injured and some were never adopted by a suitable family.

Bridget learned it was best not to check the pens down the back, where the new animals had been quarantined, and were awaiting their visit by the vet. That way, if some of them never came through to the display pens where the animals that were available for adoption were housed, Bridget remained blissfully unaware. She knew that the vet's actions were all for the best, a rabid or cancer ridden animal was in pain and required a peaceful release, but she did not like to dwell on the matter.

"I will come with you and show you which one," Jenny Lenore said. Jenny Lenore was aunt to Lena Lenore, who was in Bridget's senior class, and mother to Jamie Lenore who was in the class below. She seemed so young and pretty that few people called her 'Mrs. Lenore', just 'Jenny', but she had the kindest heart of anyone Bridget had ever met.

"I had better text my brother and tell him I'm not ready for pick-up yet," Bridget said. Her brother Fenton and his girlfriend Carlice Favor had been planning to pick her up and take her for a picnic that afternoon.

Bridget finished fiddling with her mobile phone and followed Jenny Lenore around to the rear cages. Luckily it had been a slow week for strays, and many of the cages were empty. Jenny indicated a floppy eared dog in the second cage.

"He is adorable!" Bridget exclaimed.

"The regular walker took the other dogs for their walk," Jenny explained, "But this one is shy of the other dogs, and nervous of traffic and sudden noises. That is why I thought you could walk him especially."

"I would be happy too," Bridget declared. "Does he have a name?"

"Not that I know of," Jenny said. "But I have been calling him Biggs."

"That sounds like a good name for a spaniel," Bridget said. She clipped a lead onto Biggs' collar and led him gently out of the yard. "Come along boy..."

"Remember he gets scared," Jenny called after her. "Probably been abused."

Bridget deliberately took several side lanes to spare Biggs' nerves. The streets were relatively quiet on a Saturday lunch-time anyway. After a few twists and turns she came to the school oval. Jaylen Woodgate and Javier Tilton were there, carelessly kicking around a soccer ball. Jaylen was a good player and the captain of the school football team; while Javier was his less sporty friend.

Biggs stopped and barked at Jaylen, exactly as if Jaylen was a larger dog, which Bridget found amusing because she knew that Jaylen was a wolf about four days a month, around the time when the moon was full.

"Hey," Jaylen said, coming to a halt and scooping up the ball. "What's up little brother?"

Biggs kept on barking and Bridget looked Jaylen over. His brown puppy-dog eyes sparkled and he exuded an air of canine fitness. Until a few weeks ago, Jaylen had imagined himself in love with Bridget, and hanging out with him had been fraught with certain risks, but he had recently found his ideal partner in Ivy Pinkerton.

"Calm down Biggs," Bridget soothed, tightening the spaniel's lease.

"I didn't know you had a puppy Bridget," Javier said, jogging to a halt alongside Jaylen and Biggs. He dropped to his knees beside Biggs. "Here little fella."

Biggs was immediately distracted and sniffed at Javier's hand.

"He's not mine," Bridget explained. "He's from the shelter."

"That explains the skittishness I sense," Javier said calmly. "It's all right fella." He slid a hand across the puppy's head and down its back. Biggs seemed incredibly soothed by the action.

"Jenny thought his previous owner had been cruel to him," Bridget added.

"Too many of those around unfortunately," Javier crooned. He continued to pet Biggs.

"Yeah," Bridget surveyed the boy. It was rare to see Javier without his black coat, which he seemed to tolerate summer and winter, but he had taken it off, and folded it up on one of the bleachers to play ball with Jaylen. The body underneath wasn't too bad, as Javier was wiry and rangy, and almost as tall as Damien Nevermore. She found herself admiring the cornstalk blonde hair with the straight-straight parting, and twinkling sky-blue eyes. "You are very good with animals."

"So they say," Javier said. The puppy licked his hand enthusiastically. Javier straightened self-consciously. "I'm sorry, but we better be going. Jaylen's got a date with Ivy, and I have the privilege of amusing my little sister all afternoon."

Bridget reflected that Javier's fondness for his sister Jeroma was one of his better qualities. The rest of his personality was a puzzle. He had brought big city attitudes and Goth dressing to Mystic Evermore with him from Chicago. He also studied Mandarin by correspondence and took music exams for extra credit.

When Javier had first arrived in Mystic Evermore he had an obvious crush on Lena Lenore, only reluctantly relinquishing his hopes as it became evident that Lena was getting back with Eduard Nevermore. After that, he had checked out every girl in the senior class, earning himself something of the reputation as a sleaze. Normally, Bridget did not mind a brief dance at a social with Javier, but she had never thought to encourage him to pursue a more personal relationship.

"I will see you later then," Bridget said, and tugged gently at Biggs' lease. "Come on Biggs, we got to get you back to the shelter."

Biggs cast a few longing looks back at Javier, and then slowly followed Bridget down the road. He did somehow seem a lot less nervous than earlier that day. When Jenny locked him in the cage again she observed how much good the walk had done him, and requested Bridget come by to take the young dog for a walk another day.

"I'll see what I can do," Bridget said, but she was secretly pleased, as she had taken to the dog. She texted her brother Fenton, who had been waiting to hear she was finished at the animal shelter, and a few minutes later, Fenton and Carlice arrived to pick Bridget up. They drove out to Mount Mystic, and enjoyed a picnic together in the beautiful parklands on the lower slopes.

****

Bridget did not normally volunteer at the animal shelter on Sunday, but Jenny had asked her to take Biggs for regular walks, so she stopped by the Lenore house to borrow the key to the dog yard. When she arrived, Jamie Lenore answered the door looking all muscle bound and sultry. Bridget couldn't help sneaking a second look, much to the annoyance of Jamie's secret girl-friend Raven Booth, who was lounging on the Lenore sofa.

Jamie Lenore and Raven Booth were one of Mystic Evermore's hottest couples, but they did not admit it around school, because Jamie was only a junior and Raven had been a senior until she dropped out. At school, the age and social group delineations were very strict. Seniors went out with other seniors and juniors went out with other juniors, if they were even dating yet. Jamie Lenore was something of an exception, as his physical strength was so advanced, he had caught the eye of bad-girl and sometime witch Raven Booth.

Raven uncurled from the sofa and advanced towards Bridget looking darkly beautiful and subtly dangerous. "Get your own boyfriend B----," Raven muttered, coming to lay a hand upon Jamie's muscle bound arm.

Bridget was mildly shocked, but then she remembered that amongst the African American locals some words of abuse were used in a semi-affectionate manner. "I would if I could," Bridget sighed. "You know what it is like around here Raven."

"Yeah," Raven nodded, but she still managed to sound superior. "That's why I'm so protective of my man!"

"Jenny asked me to take Biggs for a walk," Bridget ventured in an attempt to explain her presence at the Lenore house.

"Is that the new puppy?" Jamie asked with interest. "Mum's not in just now - she took Lena to the Strahan General Store." The Strahan General Store was open for two to three hours on Sunday afternoons, because Grandmother Strahan, who was also the town gossip, believed even a small town such as Mystic Evermore deserved extended shopping hours.

"I just need the key," Bridget murmured.

Jamie disappeared in the direction of his mother's bedroom, and Bridget glanced at a curiously decorated silver bowl sitting on the Lenore's coffee table. Raven followed her glance.

"I found it among my Gran's things," Raven said. "I'm not sure what it was used for." Raven had lost her Great-Grandmother the previous year in a household explosion, and Bridget had lost her mother more recently during a violent kidnapping. The high bereavement rate experienced by Mystic Evermore High Students created something of a sympathetic bond between them.

"You must miss your gran," Bridget murmured.

Raven nodded: "And you your mam..." she muttered.

"I miss her a lot," Bridget admitted. "May I look closer at your bowl?"

Raven nodded and both girls leaned together inspecting the bowl minutely.

"Gran didn't use it for grinding her herbs," Raven observed. "Or mixing her medicines."

"Perhaps it was ornamental," Bridget suggested.

"Not pushed to the back of the cupboard like it was," Raven objected.

Bridget felt in the pocket of the lightweight jacket she was wearing because the afternoon was breezy and she had expected to be outdoors with the puppy. Her fingers encountered a rounded disk, plastic in texture and much smaller than a coin. She drew the object out of her pocket and inspected it. It was one of the buttons from Damien Nevermore's white dress shirt.

Bridget clearly remembered the evening the button had come off. She had slipped out of the house for a midnight walk with Damien some weeks after her mother's death. Mum was no longer around to check up on her, and Dad was too stricken with grief to keep track of Bridget's movements like he once had. Damien was her only source of solace.

They were no longer in an official relationship, but sometimes, Damien would hold Bridget to comfort her. That evening, Bridget was crying so hard that she had soaked the front of Damien's shirt. When Damien went to unbutton the shirt and shrug it aside, one of the buttons popped off its cotton attachment.

Damien said it did not matter, he had other shirts, and besides, his tailor was sure to be able to find a spare button, but Bridget had slid the loose fastener into her pocket. In the following weeks, Bridget had forgotten what she had been wearing that night, and exactly where she had put the button. Perhaps part of her wanted it as a souvenir, a reminder that she still had the power to get Damien out of his clothes.

"I wish I was over Damien Nevermore," Bridget hissed. "I wish it was Damien feeling the pangs of unrequited love, and unable to relate to anyone else in the world." She dropped the button into Raven's Great-Grandmother's bowl in a form of ritual unburdening.

Raven looked at Bridget in alarm. "Girl that wasn't a good wish!" she said. "You should wish happiness for yourself - not pain for another. That came too close to being a hex for my liking."

Bridget shrugged. "But I'm not a witch! I don't have any sort of powers like the rest of you!"

"You said it in my presence, and I am a witch," Raven hissed. "And you dropped the button into my Gran's bowl. If that was in contact with any bodily fluids, like blood, sweat or tears - it could become a powerful charm."

"I'll take it out again then," Bridget muttered sulkily. She reached out towards the bowl, but Raven caught her hand and stilled it in mid-air.

"Stop! It doesn't work like that," Raven pronounced. "If we find you have started a hex, you can't just take the button out - you have to un-hex Damien."

"I really don't know what made me say such a thing," Bridget admitted. "I never talk about Damien anymore."

"You need to talk, girl," Raven declared with eternal wisdom. "Perhaps the bowl made you do it."

"I dunno," Bridget muttered. She was flushed and embarrassed. She was glad that Jamie arrived just then with the spare keys to the animal shelter.

"Sorry it took me so long," Jamie said. "I had to find the right set, Mum has her proper ones with her. Use this larger key, and only unlock the gates, not the building. Lock up again after yourself before, during and after your visit to the yards."

"Thanks," Bridget said, accepting the keys.

"It is essential no dogs get out, and no prowlers get in to disturb the pets," Jamie reminded her seriously.

Bridget knew that once before, the Lenores had trouble with breeders trying to get in and steal the un-neutered animals to use in their back yard breeding programs. There was no problem with the registered kennels, but some shady operators kept the animals in cruel confinement just to produce more animals to sell as pets.

"I will be responsible," Bridget promised.

Bridget left the Lenore house and walked around the block to the animal shelter. Unlocking the gate, she carefully let herself in, and locked it behind her again. Unhooking one of the leashes kept hanging in the yard, she attached it to Biggs' collar.

"Come on boy," Bridget whispered. She thought the spaniel looked pleased to see her and eager to go for a walk. Bridget fumbled with the gate lock, and once she and Biggs were outside, she locked it securely again. Biggs set off towards the park with his nose to the ground. Bridget laughed.

It was quiet in the park on a Sunday afternoon, but Bridget felt safe as long as she had Biggs with her. Biggs sniffed around and urinated under a tree. "Good boy," Bridget murmured.

"Would you say that to me?" a cheery voice asked, and Bridget craned her neck upwards to see Javier Tilton perched in a comfortable fork of the tree. It looked as though he had climbed the tree wearing his long coat and walking boots.

"Whatever are you doing there Javier?" Bridget asked.

"Photographing birds," Javier replied, and Bridget noticed the digital camera hanging from its strap on his wrist. "And reading."

"What are you reading?" Bridget asked. "More Edgar Allan Poe?"

"It's Walter de la Mare today," Javier answered.

"I think I've heard of him," Bridget mused. "Do you ever read anything more modern?"

"Like what?" Javier answered.

"Like um, err, *Hunger Games*," Bridget suggested.

"Yeah - I've read it," Javier said. "Have you?"

"I read the last one to find out how it was going to end," Bridget admitted. "Before the last movie came out."

"Ah - that tedious wait..." Javier agreed.

"Exactly," Bridget said. Biggs chose that moment to do a lump of elimination. "I'm sorry - I have to scoop that up." She pulled a plastic bag and scooper out of her jacket pocket. When the poo was safely captured, she dropped it into the garbage bin. "That's the yukky part of walking the dog."

"Yeah," Javier agreed again. "Tell me which one of the guys did you want Catniss to get together with - the soldier boy or the games hero?"

"Well at first I liked Gale, because she had always loved him," Bridget mused. "But then, I began to rather like Petyr. He had been through so much."

"Me too," Javier agreed.

"You are not looking after Jeroma today?" Bridget inquired.

"No - she went to visit with Netta Davis," Javier explained. "That gave me almost a whole day to myself."

"Cool," Bridget said. "Well I better get Biggs back to his cage. Jenny Lenore asked me to take him for a walk, but she didn't specify it had to be a long walk."

"I'm sure he has had fun, sniffing around the park, and he has relieved himself," Javier observed.

"Yes, well I will see you later then," Bridget said.

"Hey Didge," Javier called, using her hated nickname. "Would you like to go to a movie sometime?"

"No, better not," Bridget answered carelessly. "I can't seem to get into the right mood since Damien."

"You can't wait for him forever," Javier advised.

"I'm not waiting anymore," Bridget said wisely. "I'm past denial and into grief and anger."

"That's one good thing at least," Javier observed.

"Doesn't feel so good," Bridget admitted.

Bridget turned and led Biggs back towards the animal shelter. He tugged and resisted and tried to stay in the park, but Bridget was firm.

"You like Javier don't you boy?" Bridget murmured as she coaxed the reluctant puppy along. "I'm beginning to a little too."

Biggs yapped enthusiastically and Bridget laughed. "I almost swear you know what I say!" she exclaimed.

They reached the Animal Shelter and Bridget unlocked the gate. A strange man with a satchel on his back was walking down the other side of the street and Bridget locked the gate behind her hastily. It was important to be safe when you were alone in a venue. She unhooked Biggs' lease and hung it back up on the hook, keeping hold of his collar as she did do. Then she put him in his cage with a final pat.

"I will be back tomorrow or the next day, whichever I can do," Bridget promised the pup as she secured his cage. Then she unlocked the outer gate and stepped into the street. The backpacker had passed on harmlessly toward the other end of the street and probably never had been dangerous. Just a tourist - still it was best to be sure.

Bridget hurried back to the Lenore house, and knocked on the door again. This time it was Jenny Lenore who opened the door. She and Lena had returned from their short shopping trip.

"Oh Bridget," Jenny exclaimed. "How nice to see you. Jamie told me that you had taken Biggs for a walk."

"Yes, here are your spare keys," Bridget said. She held them out to Jenny, who accepted them absent-mindedly.

"Do come in for a moment," Jenny said. "I'm just unpacking the groceries, but I'm sure you deserve a drink after your walk."

"Thanks," Bridget said. She stepped in the Lenore house and the door closed behind her. "Where is Lena?"

"Lena went to her room in one of her fits of melancholy," Jenny said. A coin rolled out of her purse and dropped onto the table. Jenny picked it up and tossed it into the silver bowl on the coffee table. "It's such a responsibility looking after that girl. I often wish Lena's parents had not really been killed."

Jamie looked up from where he was reading on the sofa. "Be careful with that bowl," he said. "Apparently it belonged to Raven's grandmother."

"Granny Booth - that old witch?" Jenny scoffed.

"Exactly!" Jamie affirmed.

"Oh no Jamie dear, that is all a load of superstition," Jenny said. "Even if Grandmother Booth did mix up a few beneficial herbals, resurrection would be well beyond her powers!"

"True resurrection would have to come from God," Bridget agreed. "And you wouldn't want anything less," she added thoughtfully. Although Bridget had briefly enjoyed the company of a vampire boyfriend, she reflected that she did not really like the idea of vampire parents. In the early days of grief after her mother had died, she had wished her mother could come back, even with only a spark of life, but over time she had accepted that it was better not.

"Strange things happen around Raven, however," Jamie said. "It pays to respect the Booth ways and Booth property."

"Where is Raven now?" Bridget asked. "Has she gone home?"

"She is in Lena's room trying to comfort her," Jamie sighed. "I miss my uncle and aunt too - but some days Lena is inconsolable."

"That is only natural," Bridget said, but she did wonder a little. Lena's parents had been gone much longer than Mrs. Etheridge, and unless it took longer to mourn two parents than one, Lena ought to be moving through the various stages of grief.

"You have your father still," Jenny added almost as if she could read Bridget's mind. "He must be a great comfort to you."

"Actually Dad was very little use to anyone just after Mum died," Bridget admitted. "Fenton and I had to comfort him."

"At least you comfort each other," Jenny said. "It might have helped Lena, if she had a brother or sister even."

"She has Eduard," Bridget ventured to mention Lena's boyfriend.

"And he is a great comfort at times," Jenny said. "But a boyfriend cannot replace parents."

"And our Eduard is not as perfect as Lena thinks he is," Jamie remarked, his instinctive distrust of vampires rising to the surface. "Remember how he left her for Christy Strahan for a while?"

Lena burst out of her room briefly and glared at Jamie. "Shut up," she cried. "Fancy mentioning Christy Strahan again. Sometimes I wish you could not speak at all!"

Lena dropped a crumpled chewing gum wrapper and it hit the coffee table, somehow bouncing into the silver sugar bowl. Then she crossed to the sink and put her coffee cup and ice-cream bowl down, before retreating back into her room. Sweet snacks were often a great comfort during times of grief, and the thin girl never appeared to put on weight.

Jamie waited until the bedroom door had closed behind his cousin again and then pointed to the bowl. "Three is a charm," he said.

"I sincerely hope not," Jenny Lenore laughed. "Put that thing away in a cupboard in your room, if you are going to be superstitious about it, Jamie. That way it can't collect any more accidental objects." His mother turned to finish unpacking the groceries and then began washing up. "Bridget would you like to stay for tea tonight? Raven will be staying. We might as well make a party of it."

"Thank you Jenny," Bridget said. "But I better be getting home. Dad and Fenton need my company, and it is my turn to make our tea."

"You are such a good girl," Jenny said.

Just then Mr. Lenore entered the house from his workshop down by the garage. He gave Jenny a cute kiss and asked for a cup of tea. Seeing the two parents together gave Bridget a lump in her throat. Her Dad and Mum had been very affectionate with each other too, and now Mum was gone.

"I will see you later," Bridget said, and waved goodbye all around. Then she stepped out into the streets, hurrying to reach her home before evening fell. Mystic Evermore was not the sort of town where teenagers ought to be walking around alone at night, even if it seemed sleepy and almost perfectly safe during the day.

****

Monday morning at school, Bridget shared most of her classes with her twin brother Fenton, who was also in his senior year. Fenton usually sat with his girlfriend Carlice, unless he chose to sit with one of the guys, in which case Carlice was free to sit with Bridget. Eduard sat with his girlfriend Lena, and Jaylen Woodgate, who used to keep Bridget company, had begun sitting regularly with Ivy Pinkerton since they had been dating.

This left Bridget looking quite lonely. She could sit with Anna Vaughn, or beside Mike Davis or Javier Tilton. Mike slid into the seat beside Bridget during the first period. He was laughing and joking about football and his family doings on the weekend. Despite the fact that Mike Davis' cousin Melissa had recently married the remaining human member of the Nevermore family, Mike was the only member of the group who would not understand her feelings for a vampire.

Carlice had explained that Mike was blissfully unaware of the paranormal events surrounding the small town of Mystic Evermore, and stubbornly wished to remain that way. Once when he had begun to realize Carlices' true nature as a vampire, he had freaked out so badly that Carlice had glamoured him into forgetting everything. Now she actively protected him from being exposed to such shocking knowledge.

Mike was pretty good at ignoring the obvious and coming up with natural explanations for unnatural events. Most of the Mystic Evermore community were good at this as well. It was an important coping mechanism that contributed to their ability to live happily in the mundane world. It was a world that Damien Nevermore had wanted Bridget to rejoin, but she somehow could not.

"Err yes, Mike," Bridget murmured without taking much notice of what her companion was saying.

"You did?" Mike's eyes were glowing. "What did you think of the last kick off?"

"I'm sorry Mike," Bridget flushed at being caught out in her inattention. "I didn't mean that I actually watched the football. I um - had to work at the Animal Shelter."

"Oh yes," Mike said. "I admire you for doing your bit to help the community." His attention quickly reverted to the football. "So you missed the game?"

"I heard it was good, but I missed the actual game," Bridget admitted.

"Sometimes I miss things I want to see because I have a shift at the Snack Bar," Mike said. He began giving Bridget a blow by blow recount of the weekend football. Bridget was almost glad when she caught the teacher glaring at them.

"Shush Mike," she whispered. "Listen or we will get into trouble."

Bridget was relieved when Javier Tilton chose the seat next to her in second period. Javier's black coat and Goth make-up had make him seem like a fake and a fraud in comparison to her real vampire ex-boyfriend, Damien Nevermore. Now however, Bridget was beginning to realize there might be something special about Javier.

Despite his bizarre and sometimes macabre interests, Javier was very gentle. He looked out for his younger sister Jeroma, and rumor had it that Jaylen Woodgate had learned to control his anger issues while hanging around with Javier. Biggs seemed to be able to sniff Javier out wherever he went, and the birds up the tree had almost been eating out of Javier's hand Sunday afternoon.

"Hey," Bridget whispered shyly.

"Do you mind if I sit here?" Javier asked.

Bridget shook her head. "You are welcome." As late as last week she might have made an excuse, or perhaps hinted that the seat was saved for one of the girls.

Javier slid into the seat. "How's your morning been so far?"

"Good," Bridget murmured. She had served her father and brother breakfast cereal; packed Dad a lunch - because otherwise he would forget, and set off to school with Fenton. She did not bother to elaborate.

Javier liked to listen in class, so he was actually a relaxing seat mate.

Recess time Bridget ran into Jamie Lenore on her way to the senior locker area. "Hello Jamie," she called.

Jamie coughed and pointed to his throat.

Bridget stopped walking. "What?" she asked.

"I woke up this morning with laryngitis," Jamie wheezed.

"Shouldn't you be in bed?" Bridget inquired.

Jamie shook his head. "No fever," he wheezed.

Bridget remembered the silver bowl. "It is odd that you should have lost your voice just after your cousin made that wish," she said.

Jamie shrugged. "Coincidence?" he wheezed.

Bridget hurried to the locker area and collected her books for the next class. Arriving at the room early, she sat beside Carlice, forcing her brother to find another seat mate. Fenton sat beside Jaylen, who was alone because Ivy was sitting with Christy Strahan. Christy was Ivy's best friend, but she only attended school when she felt like it, today must have been one of her better days.

The classes were pretty average and Bridget filled several pages with notes. Her stomach rumbled, reminding her that lunch time was looming. She was sitting in sight of the wall clock and could not help glancing up at its hands every few minutes. At last the lecture was over and the senior students were free.

Bridget was on her way to the picnic table in the school ground that her friends often shared. It was just isolated enough to give the group a little privacy, which was greatly valued as not only were they normal, hormone driven teenagers, they harbored a number of secrets between them. As she approached the table, she was surprised to see the darkly brooding presence of Damien Nevermore, sprawled on the bench seat.

"What's up?" Bridget said, coming to a halt beside the table.

Damien rose to his feet. "We need to go for a walk Bridget," he said.

"I want to stay right here," Bridget replied firmly. Her days of tarrying with Damien Nevermore were over.

Damien sighed. "Raven says it is possible you put this on me," he began. "If you did - I beg of you to take it away."

"Whatever is it?" Bridget demanded.

"Well I went past my Uncle's house this morning before breakfast and Netta Davis was visiting his wife Melissa," Damien said. "I'm horribly ashamed to say that as I was talking to Sebastian, I got this painful wave of romantic feeling for Netta. Imagine - a junior - how horribly inappropriate!"

Damien Nevermore had been a young man around twenty when he was turned into a vampire. His body had remained young, and he occasionally allowed himself to date high school seniors, who were physically appropriate for him. But as his mind had matured beyond his body over the years, he often found himself more comfortable with mature women, such as Carlice's mother, Sarah Favor, whom he had also dated briefly. He had never in all his undead life allowed himself to look at a high school junior. Although they were only one year younger than seniors, Damien drew a very strict line.

"So what happened?" Bridget inquired.

"Nothing," Damien said. "I said goodbye and forced myself to leave. However, I am tortured with feelings of longing and inappropriate images in my head. I feel like a dirty pedophile."

"Netta is not that young, you know," Bridget objected.

"I expect not," Damien said. "But it is against my principles. To make things worse, Netta has had a crush on my younger brother Eduard for some time. Eduard doesn't encourage her because he has Lena - but he is protective of her."

Bridget began to crack a smile. "It sounds like unrequited love to me."

"I don't believe these feelings arose spontaneously within me," Damien declared. "I ran into Raven Booth when I was feeling all nauseous and woozy, and she told me about your revenge wish."

"Yeah sorry about that," Bridget flushed.

"I apologize if I hurt you so much that you need revenge, Bridget," Damien said. "I thought we had been good together up to a certain point. And then I felt it better to set you free. No one wants to see a burden like me permanently with a nice young girl like you. We agreed on that."

"Yes - but we didn't agree that you would move on with Carlice's mother," Bridget declared bitterly.

"I haven't," Damien declared desperately. "My history with Sarah Favor is long and complicated."

"I heard Raven's name," Jamie Lenore wheezed, coming up behind Bridget. Jamie didn't always eat with the seniors as he was a junior, but he was part of their friendship group.

"Damien thinks my curse on him came true!" Bridget explained. "He now has an inappropriate crush on someone."

"And I can't speak," Jamie wheezed.

Bridget and Jamie turned to look at each other. "If two out of three wishes have come true..." Bridget murmured.

"Mum's wish!" Jamie gasped. "We have to get to the cemetery."

"What?" Damien was puzzled.

"Do you have your car here Damien?" Bridget asked. "Jenny Lenore wished that Lena's parents 'weren't really dead'."

"Oh-uh, that could be trouble," Damien Nevermore agreed. He turned and led the way to where his car had been parked in the visitor's car park. Javier and Jaylen, who had been approaching the lunch table, followed them. "Get in," Damien said. He frowned, "You three boys in the back put on your seatbelts please. I had them installed especially."

"Shut up and just drive Damien," Jamie cried.

Luckily they did not run into any of the county police on the way to the cemetery. Nor did they have an accident. Everyone piled out of the car and Jamie set off at a run towards where his uncle and aunt had been buried. The others followed, catching up when Jamie skidded to a halt.

"Too late!" Jamie cried.

The group crowded around, staring at the grave in horror. It looked as though something, or several somethings had tunneled out recently. A neat cylindrical hole wound its way out of the grave into the grass above somewhat like a giant worm hole, and a bunch of fading flowers had been scattered as if by the passage of an animal.

Jamie touched the exposed earth: "I don't sense vampires," he said.

"Nor do I," Damien said. "However, according to legend, if the dead are called back by voodoo magic, they become zombies - not vampires."

"Zombies?" Bridget was horrified by the thought of the ravening, decaying, mindless flesh-eating creatures of modern film. "Like in the movies?"

Damien shook his head. "Not like that," he said. "Zombies are commonly the silent servants of the person who conjured them. They are single-minded about their mission and will not rest until they have accomplished it."

"Where do you think they went?" Jamie asked.

"Possibly to Jenny Lenore for their instructions," Damien said.

"I'm off home," Jamie exclaimed. "You guys try the animal shelter!" Jamie broke into a run, his super-charged hunter's limbs covering the ground with unnatural speed.

Damien led Bridget, Javier and Jaylen back to his car. The polished vintage model gleamed in the cemetery car park, as everyone climbed inside. Damien started the engine and drove around to the animal shelter, which was open during business hours on a Monday of course.

Jenny Lenore was at the front desk filing some receipts. She looked up in surprise and disapproval. "What are you kids doing here during school hours?" she exclaimed.

"Could you close up for a few minutes?" Bridget asked.

Jenny frowned. "I don't know," she said.

"It's a serious matter and possibly one of public safety," Damien said, using a persuasive tone.

"All right then," Jenny said. "Just till this has been sorted out." Jenny wore a verbena necklace that Lena had given her one Christmas, so she had some resistance to Damien's charisma, but she was still mildly convinced. She swung the open sign on the door around to closed, and engaged the latch. "Now what is it?"

"Do you remember throwing a coin into Grandmother Booth's silver bowl and wishing?" Bridget began.

Jenny frowned. "Of course not!" Jenny said. "I don't believe in wishes."

"I was there," Bridget said patiently. "A coin fell out of your purse..."

"Yes, I remember that," Jenny said. "And I put it in the old bowl for safe keeping."

"And your exact words were - sometimes I wish..." Bridget explained.

"Yeah, but I didn't mean anything. I was just off-loading," Jenny said.

"Well three people off-loaded yesterday, and today Jamie can't talk, Damien is under a love spell and there is a hole in Lena's parents grave," Bridget explained.

Jenny Lenore looked frightened. "That is unnatural," she said. "This is going to be one of those horrible things I don't understand - isn't it?"

"I hope not ma'am," Damien said. "Is there any chance we can go around the back?"

"Sure," Jenny led the way into the yard. "It is more private here. So when are we expecting - whatever we are expecting?"

"Any moment now," Damien said. "Jamie went to check your house."

A dozen puppies yipped and whined, sensing Jaylen's wolfy presence. He and Javier went into the dog cages to greet and sooth them. There was a knocking at the outer gate. Everyone jumped. It wasn't Lena's parents, however, it was Mrs. Grey, looking for her pet-of-the-day.

"Why is the shelter closed?" Mrs. Grey shouted.

Jenny shrugged helplessly and Bridget approached the gate. "We are cleaning the cages," Bridget replied.

"So why can't I come inside?" Mrs. Grey demanded.

"Temporary quarantine," Bridget said. "We are waiting for the vet to visit. Please come another day Mrs. Grey."

Mrs. Grey muttered angrily, using a few words she ought not to use around people or animals. Then she fell silent and began to back away hastily. Bridget looked up and noticed two figures approaching. The figures did not speak, and they walked rigidly upright with unnatural rhythm. They wore long coats and wide brimmed hats purloined from the hall-stand at the Lenore house. The hats were stored there for summer, while the coats were reserved for winter. The combination was bizarre and unnatural, as was the glimpse of what lay beneath.

Lena's parents had been buried for more than a year now. However, in a sealed coffin deep in cold soil in a relatively cool climate, decomposition had occurred gradually, and there was something almost recognizable about them still. They caught hold of the outer gate and rattled its bars.

Bridget did not expect the zombies to be able to speak, but they voiced words hoarsely. "Jenny," the female Zombie cried. "Jenny Lenore."

Jenny Lenore was fainting from fear. She screwed her eyes shut and hid her face in Damien's broad chest. Bridget thought bitterly that a number of mature women appeared to find her vampire ex-boyfriend's presence very comforting.

"This is not happening," Jenny sobbed. "I cannot look! I must be hallucinating. Grief does funny things to the human mind."

"They won't go away until you give them their instructions," Damien Nevermore said. "If Lena's parents were really here - what would you want them to do Jenny? Be careful what you say!"

"Help Lena," Jenny sobbed. "Comfort Lena. It has been so hard looking after here since they passed."

The zombies turned and strutted jerkily away, almost comically arm-in-arm. They had their orders. Jenny Lenore collapsed, as she was shaking with fear. Damien carried her gently out to the car, while Bridget called Javier and Jaylen out of the dog compound. Then she checked that the animal shelter was fully locked behind them.

Damien called ahead on his mobile phone to warn his brother Eduard, who would most likely be with Lena Lenore, to expect zombie visitors.

"Get Lena out of the school and to some less populated area," Damien cried. "Her parents are coming to help and comfort her - and I don't think they mean to do her history project for her!"

Damien drove back to the Lenore house, where Jamie was waiting. Together they put Jenny Lenore to bed and gave her the headache tablet she asked for. Because Jenny was the one who had called the vampires, she was not in a lot of danger, except from her own fear. However, Jamie called Raven and asked her to come over and advise them what to do.

****

A few minutes later Raven Booth arrived at the Lenore house. She hugged Jamie Lenore and gave him a kiss. Then she greeted Jaylen, Bridget, Damien and Javier. "I'm so sorry my bowl caused this," Raven gushed.

"You weren't to know people would actually throw things into it and wish," Jamie wheezed.

"We will have to do something about your voice," Raven said.

"And my inappropriate love spell," Damien said sternly. "However, the first thing is - how do you get rid of zombies?"

"Um," Raven said, "It's not normally the sort of magic I deal in - but you destroy the corn dolly."

Damien shook his head. "There are no dolls," he observed.

"Hmm no," Raven admitted. "Perhaps fire?"

Jamie looked indignant. "We can't possibly burn my uncle and aunt!" he exclaimed. "They didn't even ask for this."

Raven thought long and hard. "Some people believe that the soul will eventually fade," she said. "So the problem would go away if you could keep them from doing any harm for long enough."

Damien frowned. "Babysit zombies?" he exclaimed. "For how long?"

"I'm not sure," Raven said. "Like I said - even when I touch the dark side of magic - a little self-defense perhaps - I prefer to not to interfere with

71

the dead. Nature has its laws and there is a natural cycle which should be left alone."

"Understood," Damien said.

"Is there a way we could hurry Lena's parent's return to oblivion?" Bridget inquired. She had always been taught that the dead should rest peacefully until the end of time. Of course, one should not mix legend and theology.

"Perhaps if you could make them believe their mission is complete..." Raven mused.

Damien Nevermore demanded Jamie fetch the silver bowl from the cupboard and picked up the coin Jenny Lenore had used to wish. He wrapped it carefully in a clean handkerchief and slipped it into his top pocket. "It might be helpful," he said.

Damien frowned at his own shirt button which had lain in the silver bowl beside the coin, but did not touch it. Inconvenient revenge love hexes could wait until later. It was the return of Lena's parents from the grave which was most unnatural and possibly the most dangerous. This problem would require solving first.

"I'm staying here to look after my mother," Jamie Lenore said.

Damien nodded. "That's just as well," he said. As a hereditary vampire hunter, Jamie had unnatural strength that would assist him in the event of a confrontation with the zombies. However, Mrs. Lenore would most likely only be in danger if the zombies returned to ask for more instructions and she lost her head in fear.

"I will keep Jamie company," Jaylen said. A werewolf bite did not seem to be required anywhere, but he could tell his friend needed moral support.

"Good idea," Damien said. He expected Javier, who was normally best friends with Jaylen, to volunteer to stay as well, but Javier remained stubbornly close to Bridget.

"I'm coming to make sure Bridget is okay," Javier said.

Damien Nevermore frowned. He had broken up with Bridget and advised her to move on with a human boyfriend. However, Damien privately believed no local youth was good enough for Bridget and had not expected to face a rival for some years. Javier Tilton on the other hand, once claimed not to be afraid of Damien Nevermore, and proved it by standing face to face with the vampire as he began to turn vampiric.

"Okay," Damien said. He didn't think things had progressed very far between Javier and Bridget at this stage anyway. "Perhaps your skills could be of some use." Javier's ability to calm animals, and even occasionally vampires was outstanding. "Everyone in the car!"

Raven, Bridget and Javier jumped into Damien Nevermore's car and the group drove toward the park beside the river.

Eduard had texted Damien, telling him that Lena had lured her zombie parents into a sheltered area on the far bank. Damien parked the car and everyone got out. They walked past the community gardens and across the footbridge, to find Lena sitting on the grassy slope of the river bank facing her parents.

Eduard, who had been hovering nearby, greeted Damien.

"Lena has been amazing," Eduard reported. "She cried, but she did not seem frightened of them. Their ability to talk is limited, but they seem harmless. They just keep trying to comfort Lena and make her happy."

"We will be lucky if that is all that happens," Damien said grimly.

"Yeah," Raven agreed. "The reason why witches ought not to bring people back from the dead is they aren't the same - ever. Who can tell what is safe or right?"

"As we know," Bridget said, "This was an accident and Jenny Lenore's intentions were completely innocent."

"That may help," Raven admitted. "But I would be surprised if comforting Lena is all her parents try to do."

"What do you mean?" Bridget asked.

"Well what if they take things a bit further and try to take her home to look after her themselves?" Raven suggested.

"That doesn't sound too bad," Javier said. "Although it might frighten Jenny and Mr. Lenore some more."

"Think," Raven insisted. "Where exactly would Lena's parents think home was?"

"I don't know," Javier said. "They were dead before I moved to town. Their old house maybe?"

"Their old house has now been rented to the Etheridges," Raven said.

"I expect my Dad could cope," Bridget said. "He does know a few of the town secrets and is equipped to deal with the unnatural to a certain extent."

"The zombies facing Captain Etheridge and his army issue secret weapons would be too convenient," Damien said. "Where else might they think of as home - now they are dead?"

"Oh," Bridget exclaimed. "I see what you mean. The cemetery."

"More specifically - their graves," Raven added.

"I don't think Lena wants to go there," Bridget said frowning. Lena Lenore was not her favorite person in the whole world, indeed Lena could be somewhat rude at times, but she would not wish anything horrible upon her. Certainly nothing like being tugged down into a grave in the earth.

"So we have got to solve the problem before evening falls," Damien said. "Assuming her parents try to go back to bed like normal parents at that time. One can never be sure, but the Zombie Lenores are acting like they retain some basic instincts and memories."

"What can we do?" Eduard asked.

However, Damien did not answer. He was staring off into space. "Netta would be getting home from school just now," he murmured. "I hope she is all right."

Eduard gave Damien a puzzled look. "The afternoon is bringing us bigger problems than our aunt's little cousin man," Eduard said. "What is wrong with you?"

"Damien got slightly hexed too," Bridget explained. "My fault - we will deal with it later."

"Earth to Damien," Eduard said, and gave his brother a slight shake.

Just then, a cloud passed over the sun and the area beside the river became quite dull. The zombie parents, who had been quite content so long as they were talking to their daughter, suddenly became anxious. They stood up and took Lena's hands, indicating she ought to go with them.

Lena glanced back at Eduard for guidance. Eduard shook his head. "Don't go with them Lena."

Lena's parents began pulling at Lena impatiently. Eduard and Damien took hold of the parents and tried to pull them off Lena. The vampires were unnaturally strong, but on the other hand, the zombies were compelled. They really believed their mission included taking their daughter back to the grave for the night. They hung on until their old bones creaked.

Damien and Eduard let go of Lena's parents. "We don't want to traumatize Lena by pulling her parent's arms off in front of her," Eduard observed.

Lena reluctantly took one or two steps in the direction her parents wanted.

"Let me have a go," Javier said. He stepped between the zombie parents and the direction of the cemetery. "You want to stay in this lovely park and talk to your daughter," he intoned in his most hypnotic voice.

The parents hesitated, but they clearly were not convinced. Javier repeated his persuasions. "This is a beautiful park and you were helping Lena so nicely. You want to sit down again..." he said.

The parents stopped pulling Lena along, but they did not sit down. They remained confused. After a few minutes, the zombie father glanced anxiously in the direction of the cemetery again. The zombie mother followed his gaze.

Javier changed his strategy and tried a new argument. "It is not evening yet," he said, pointing to the sky.

Luckily the cloud cover moved along just then, and the remains of the afternoon sun shone down on the park. The zombie parents relaxed immediately and sat down on the grass again facing Lena. They clasped her hands and gazed at her intently.

"Daughter," the Zombie Father rasped. "We miss you."

"I miss you too Daddy," Lena wept. "I missed you and Mummy so much."

"Who look?" the Zombie Mother attempted to creak.

"Aunt Jenny looks after me now," Lena explained.

"Jenny - yes - Jenny," the Zombie Father rasped. "Sister Jenny."

"Jenny call us," the Zombie Mother creaked.

"You see what we will be dealing with," Eduard said softly to the others. "As soon as sunset falls they will try to take Lena again."

"It is hard to reach their decayed minds," Javier said. "I'm not sure I can solve your problem."

"It would help if you stopped day-dreaming Damien," Eduard was used to depending on his older brother and sounded frustrated.

"I've been helping all day," Damien said. "In fact, I was on the case before you were."

"But now your mind is everywhere," Eduard complained. "What sort of spell is this? One that makes you go and check on random people?"

"Something like that," Bridget murmured.

"Check on Netta," Damien muttered. "It's a very good idea." He patted his top pocket and seemed to notice the bulge of his handkerchief. "You might need this!" Damien handed his clean folded handkerchief to Eduard. Then he strode off in the direction of his car.

Eduard stared at Damien's handkerchief in astonishment. "What would I want Damien's handkerchief for?" he exclaimed.

"I think I remember something," Bridget said. "Let me have that." She carefully unfolded the handkerchief to expose the coin. "This is the coin Jenny used to wish for the return of Lena's parents."

Eduard looked annoyed. "This could be useful," he said. "Why didn't Damien bring it out before?"

"His mind is a bit affected too," Bridget explained. "Like I said - my fault."

"Give me the coin," Raven said. "I'm not sure this will work, but it is worth a try." She handed the handkerchief containing the coin to Lena. "Tell your parents that they have helped and comforted you," she instructed. "Then give them the coin."

"Oh!" Lena gasped. She turned to her zombie parents. "Mum and Dad - it's been lovely talking to you."

"S-lovely," wheezed the Zombie Father.

"You have helped me a lot," Lena said. "You have fulfilled your task. You can go in peace now."

For an instant, the teens feared the plan would not work, but then the zombie father took the coin. "Be happy," the Zombie Father wheezed.

"I will," Lena assured him. "And this is my boyfriend Eduard."

"Eduard," the Zombie Mother creaked. "We have to leave now."

The zombie parents turned and ambled awkwardly across the bridge to the other side of the river. Then they turned in the direction of the cemetery. Their progress was slow, but determined. Eduard gathered Lena to him in a big hug.

"I'm sorry you had to go through that Lena," he said.

"I'm not," Lena said. "In a funny sort of way - it did help me. They clearly were not themselves - but I had been missing them horribly. Almost morbidly. This gave me a chance to say goodbye. And I'm glad they met you."

"That's something," Eduard said.

"Damien took his car," Raven said. "Do you have your here Eduard?"

"Yes," Eduard said. "Although I'm not sure I can fit everybody. It's a sports model."

"I'm coming with you," Raven said. "I need to cleanse the Lenore house and make sure there are no ill after effects on Jenny Lenore."

"I will walk Bridget back to her house, if that is all right by Bridget," Javier said.

"I would appreciate that Javier," Bridget said. She had been impressed by Javier's kind persuasion of Lena's parents, when even the Nevermore brothers' vampire strength had failed to solve the problem.

Eduard, Lena and Raven climbed into Eduard's vintage car and roared off in the direction of the Lenore house. Now the crisis was over, Lena was keen to be re-united with the living members of her family, and make sure they were well.

****

Javier turned to Bridget. "If you don't mind Bridget," he said, "I would like to hold your hand and get out of here as quickly as possible. It is creepy with evening falling after what happened."

"I agree," Bridget said. She extended her hand to Javier and they began to walk towards town and their respective homes. "You were great," she exclaimed. "What was that - hypnotism?"

"I prefer to call it hypnotism in public," Javier said. "Because people accept and believe in hypnotherapy to a certain extent."

"But you can do more?" Bridget murmured.

"I can communicate with animals," Javier explained. "Wolves primarily. My powers of persuasion over vampires, zombies and people are just the overflow of my primary function."

"Is there a name for your powers?" Bridget asked.

"Jaylen and Damien call me a 'wolf whisperer'," Javier replied.

The teens noticed a vintage car parked alongside the road in the next street.

"Is that Damien's car?" Javier inquired.

"Yeah," Bridget said. "It's outside the Davis house."

"Damien was acting a bit weird - do you think he could be causing trouble?" Javier asked.

"I honestly don't know," Bridget said. "The Davises and Nevermore's are related by marriage now."

Damien and Mike Davis appeared on the front porch, outlined in the light streaming from the front door. They were talking earnestly, almost arguing. Bridget knew that Mike stubbornly refused to accept Damien's vampire nature, and would not be comfortable with Damien hanging around their house too much.

"I had better get this," Bridget whispered.

"I know he is your ex-boyfriend and all that," Javier said. "But it strikes me you could use a hand with him."

"Okay," Bridget whispered. She was half relieved. She had been alone in the morass of her feelings for Damien Nevermore for months.

"It was nice of you to stop by and give the flowers to Mum," Mike was saying. "But I do hope you are not planning to start courting her now - like you did Carlice's mum!"

"Not your mother," Damien was clearly struggling to say something appropriate.

"Melissa joined your family," Mike said practically. "We are a bit more distant."

Bridget and Javier stepped out of the shadows. "It was my idea Mike," Bridget said.

Mike's face cleared as he viewed Bridget. "Please take Damien away Bridget," he said. "To be honest, he's getting a bit stalky. And I think he must be drunk. He keeps starting sentences and not finishing them."

"None of this is quite what you think Mike!" Bridget said. "It was a Lenore family matter. The rest of us were helping."

"We are not part of the Lenore family," Mike said.

Bridget shrugged. "It's a small town," she said. "What affects one, affects all."

"It sure does," Mike agreed somewhat cynically. "But you know I like to keep out of all the drama."

"Get into the car, Damien," Bridget said, giving her ex-boyfriend a friendly shove. Damien responded by climbing into the driver's seat. But then he just sat there unable to drive.

"He is getting worse," Mike observed.

"I can drive," Javier said. "Help me push Damien across to the passenger seat Mike."

Mike Davis helped Javier shift Damien Nevermore across to the passenger side of his own vehicle. Then Javier got into the driver's seat. Bridget climbed into the rear of the car.

"Keys please man," Javier said. Damien meekly handed the car keys across.

"Careful - vintage," he stammered.

"I know, it's a beauty," Javier said. "Where to man?"

"Nevermore Manor," Bridget said firmly.

Javier turned the key in the ignition and allowed the motor a moment to warm up, then he pulled gently away from the front of the Davis house. "I've been to the Manor a couple of times," he said. "I think I can find it."

"Eduard probably won't be home," Bridget said. "He was going to stay at the Lenore's."

"So we are alone with the big bad," Javier said. "Do you think we can manage?"

"Lock me in the basement," Damien said. "So I don't try to get out and climb into Netta's window, or sing love songs outside her porch. This spell is giving me so many weird ideas."

"I hope you don't start feeling suicidal," Bridget exclaimed.

"So do I," Damien said. "But I think that stage would take a while to develop. Lock me in the basement and then call your dad, Bridget."

"I would rather take the hex off you," Bridget objected.

"Captain Etheridge may have some ideas," Damien said. "Besides, he needs to know where his daughter is, and with whom."

"I must admit, I wouldn't mind having an adult around," Javier admitted, as he drove into the driveway of Nevermore Manor. "Normally Damien counts as one, but not in that condition."

"Nice one, man," Damien agreed wryly.

Damien climbed out of the car and unlocked the front door, before leading the way to the stairs leading down to the lower level. There was an area that had been fitted out as a bunker. Once locked, it was safe from both the outside and the inside.

"I don't like to lock you inside," Bridget wailed.

"There's a television, and bed and even refrigerator full of supplies," Damien said. "I suspect the spell affects me worse at night - I kept my mind off Netta for quite a while during the day. I will be alright."

"You know I'm here, man," Javier said. "Perhaps I could help."

"Thanks," Damien said. "But if whisperer powers were able to reverse love spells, the legends would have said so! Love spells are particularly nasty. That's why most witches won't perform them. Spells to enhance existing love are okay, and spells to help you find your true love are fine -

but not spells to force love against your will!"

"I'm so sorry," Bridget sobbed. "I have done a bad thing."

"I probably deserved it," Damien groaned. He stepped into the bunker and Javier slammed the door shut. Then the wolf-whisperer turned the key in the outside of the lock.

"Call your Dad, Bridget," Javier said. "And let's go upstairs to the lounge to wait for him."

"But Damien..." Bridget began.

"Damien is exactly where he wants to be at the moment," Javier said. "And I know he is strong, he would not have allowed us to put him there, if it were not for the best."

When Captain Etheridge arrived at Nevermore Manor about half-an-hour later, he was accompanied by Sheriff Favor. The Captain noticed that Bridget cast a resentful glance towards the Sheriff, and hastened to justify the woman's presence.

"This is the Sheriff's town and I work closely with her," Captain Etheridge observed sternly. "Besides, I know that she cares about Damien Nevermore."

"Whatever happened?" Sarah Favor inquired.

"I was upset and I wished Damien would feel the pain of unrequited love," Bridget admitted. "Unfortunately, I did not know that the silver bowl really was a wishing bowl, and I dropped one of Damien's shirt buttons into the bowl."

It was embarrassing and humiliating for Bridget to admit to her rival the depths of her agony over Damien, but Sarah Favor merely laughed and patted Bridget on the shoulder.

"Sometimes I have been very angry with Damien myself," the Sheriff agreed. "If my wishes had power then... anything could have happened."

"Yeah," Bridget was still somewhat embarrassed.

"Now I think it might be better if I never know who Damien has been cursed to love," the Sheriff continued.

Bridget was vastly relieved. "I think so too," she gasped. "I'm sure it was just a random thing. Someone he was visiting at the time."

"Is there any chance that true love could cure this?" the Captain asked.

Sheriff Favor blushed. "I'm not sure I am ready for my love for Damien to be true love," she exclaimed.

"He has been with me all day and that did not fix anything," Bridget announced angrily.

"You have a lot of unresolved issues with Damien, so your love probably is not true at the moment," Sheriff Favor said. "And I have been angry with him for months, so my love has not been true."

"Does it have to be romantic love?" Captain Etheridge inquired. "Perhaps Eduard's love for his brother is true?"

"No - the brother's fight all the time," Bridget said.

"What about Sebastian Nevermore?" Sarah Favor suggested. "He chose to adopt the boys, although he fully knew what they were."

"It is very possible Sebastian's love is true," Captain Etheridge said. "But with his wife pregnant, I am reluctant to call him away from home at this hour. Let me research the details of the spell, and we will call Sebastian in the morning."

"So Damien stays in the bunker until morning?" Bridget asked.

"The bunker is comfortable enough," Captain Etheridege said. He turned to Javier Tilton. "Your parents will be looking for you, boy."

The Captain insisted Javier get into his car and be driven home for the night. Bridget was left in the company of the Sheriff, until Captain Etheridge returned. Sheriff Favor and Bridget went and peeked into the bunker through the close circuit television. Damien Nevermore was scribbling something on a piece of paper, and by the way the lines did not reach the edge of the paper, the women assumed he was writing poetry. Then he stopped and paced for a while. After that, he turned the television on and whiled away the time watching some sentimental old movie.

"He doesn't appear that dangerous," Bridget ventured.

"Remember his phenomenal strength," Sarah Favor murmured.

Sure enough, Damien tired of his incarceration and began to bang on the bunker door. However, the vault was especially designed to keep a vampire in or out as required. Although Damien had been locked away by his own suggestion, his face began to bunch up, and his fangs appeared. The frustrations caused by the spell were beginning to wear away at even Damien Nevermore's pristine control.

Captain Etheridge had returned with take-away pizza, which Bridget and Sheriff Favor ate hungrily. When Damien was civilly offered a slice, he just snarled, however. The Captain frowned, and suggested that Bridget try to get some sleep as Tuesday was a school day. Bridget stretched out on the sofa in the spare lounge, and listened to the gentle murmur of voices as her father and Sheriff Favor talked.

Bridget woke early in the morning and checked on the close-circuit television. Damien had tired himself out and was sleeping uncomfortably, messily surrounded by some packaged blood he had removed from the bunker refrigerator and microwaved for himself. The discarded plastic was strewn around the room, and stains of brown were smeared around his normally handsome mouth. His curly hair was not just naturally tousled, but tangled by frequently running frustrated fingers through it.

Damien was a long way from the suave, well dressed lover Bridget had always encountered. Except for the times that he had nobly sacrificed himself in battle to save Bridget and her friends, she had never even seen Damien disheveled. Bridget reflected it was perhaps good for her to see this less attractive side of Damien. It might reduce his fascination for her and help her move on with a human boy.

Captain Etheridge had been out and picked up muffins for their breakfast. He had also collected a fresh school uniform from their home. He told Bridget and the Sheriff that they were expecting Sebastian Nevermore at any moment. Her brother Fenton had a normal night at home the previous evening and sent his love. Fenton hoped everything would work out for Damien, and that Bridget would get over the bitterness which made her cast the wish.

Sebastian Nevermore arrived with his wife Melissa. Bridget had always wondered whether Melissa Nevermore knew her husband's so-called nephews were vampires, but she seemed to understand as she viewed the close circuit television screen. Melissa was now a few months pregnant and her pregnancy was beginning to show.

"I will have to go down there to him dear," Sebastian said.

Melissa nodded. "He looks terrible," she said.

"Are you sure you will be alright?" Captain Etheridge asked anxiously. He produced a set of silver handcuffs: "Do you need these?"

"I think I can manage without weapons," Sebastian Nevermore said. "But you may come with me if you wish Captain. That way if Damien does get out of hand, you can help restrain him."

"As you wish, Sebastian," Captain Etheridge said.

"You might need this," Bridget said, shamefacedly offering up the button from Damien's shirt. After Damien had looked through the contents of the silver bowl the previous afternoon, Bridget had quietly pocketed the token. She had done this half out of shame, and half in the knowledge that it would be useful for breaking the spell over Damien.

"Thanks," Sebastian said. He did not ask what the significance of the button was, or why Bridget had it, but simply pocketed it. Sebastian Nevermore was clearly a man of action rather than words, who took things as they presented themselves to him.

The two men turned and headed down the stairs towards the cellar and the bunker, while the three women clustered around the close-circuit television. Sebastian and Captain Etheridge knocked politely on the cellar door, even though it was locked from the outside. Damien woke with a start.

"Is it morning?" Damien muttered blearily.

"It is morning, Damien," Captain Etheridge replied. "May we come inside?"

"Who do you have with you?" Damien asked cautiously. His teeth were retracting, and his face was returning to its usual handsome outlines, but he retained an edginess that was not normal for him.

"Your Uncle Sebastian," Captain Etheridge replied.

"Okay," Damien agreed. He began to hastily tidy the bunker, tucking the plastic wrappers into the small bin. Then he sat down to wait for his visitors.

Captain Etheridge unlocked the bunker door and stepped inside, along with Sebastian Nevermore. Sebastian stepped towards his adopted nephew, and pulled up a kitchen-style chair in order to sit opposite Damien on the sofa.

"How are you, Nephew?" Sebastian asked.

"I've been better, Uncle," Damien replied. "I don't know whether the Captain has told you, but Bridget in her pain, cast a love spell on me, so that I would feel unrequited longing too."

"It sounds nasty," Sebastian said.

"It is," Damien said. "It is not appropriate for me to approach the object of my affection, who is completely innocent of the spell. So I'm suffering all the pangs of extreme infatuation."

"Horrible," Sebastian said.

"The spell has stirred up the blood thirst too," Damien admitted. "For the first time in some fifty years, I am afraid I might hurt someone. I am surprised that you would risk being here with me!"

Damien began to cry, and Sebastian handed him a handkerchief. He also continued to eye his adopted nephew with the utmost trust and kindness.

"The love of family means so much at a time like this," Damien sobbed.

"I know, that's why I am here," Sebastian said.

"But I am not your nephew, like we tell the world," Damien sobbed. "I'm more like your grandmother's great-uncle or something."

"In our hearts, we are exactly what we decided to be," Sebastian said. "My human age makes me your senior relative today. And I couldn't bear to leave you and Eduard unacknowledged, once I had discovered the connection."

"You have a big heart Sebastian," Damien said. "Anyone else would have left Eduard and me to take care of ourselves, we have knocked around homeless in the past."

"I didn't want you two homeless, or even in a strange home," Sebastian murmured. "You belong in Mystic Evermore with me!"

"But this has cost you Sebastian," Damien sobbed. "Melissa might not have been attacked by the bear, if it had not been for me."

"I love Melissa dearly and would never wish any pain on her," Sebastian said. "But I cannot blame you for the bear attack. I lost my parents in mysterious circumstances too, and that was not your fault."

"More like a Nevermore family curse," Damien said. "My presence can only make it worse."

"I don't believe that," Sebastian said.

Damien glanced around. "Someone should get Raven Booth," he said. "So she can work on breaking this spell."

"The Captain suggested that true love might break the spell," Sebastian said. He handed Damien the button from his shirt. "Bridget sends her forgiveness, and I am offering you the truest family love that I can," he said. "All you have to do is accept it."

Damien took the button and ground it to dust between his fingers. "Oh uncle," he groaned and allowed Sebastian Nevermore to enclose him in a great human hug. "I love you too."

Nothing visibly changed, but there seemed to be a brief brightness around Damien's figure, and a general relaxation of tension. The vampire youth continued to allow Sebastian to hug him. Both uncle and nephew cried a few manly tears.

Sheriff Sarah Favor was also crying. "Why couldn't I love Damien like that?" she sobbed. "When I found out he was a vampire - I got angry and felt used. I suspected he was a threat to community security, and blamed him for a few local crimes, which I have since discovered he did not commit."

"Hush Sarah," Melissa said, hugging her friend. "Trust between a man and a woman takes time to develop. Even true love takes time to develop."

Sarah Favor wiped her eyes. "Please don't tell Damien I was here," she whispered. Then the Sheriff turned to Bridget. "Didge, please ask your father not to mention me either. I don't want Damien to know that I was here and failed him."

Sheriff Favor walked out of the room and towards the front door of the Manor. Melissa and Bridget heard the door open and close softly behind the woman. The patrol car hummed into life and purred out down the drive.

"I think the Sheriff really does love Damien," Melissa mused. "But she is not ready to tell him yet."

"I think something like that too," Bridget said.

Captain Etheridge came up the stairs. "Bridget," he said. "I think Damien might be cured! Now you have to have a quick shower, and get into that clean uniform I brought you. I intend to drive you to school straight away."

"Aw - Dad," Bridget complained, but it was no use. The Captain was adamant. Tuesday was a school day and Bridget was a senior student. It was important for her to attend regularly.

****

Bridget was pleased to see her twin brother Fenton when she arrived at school. Public displays of affection between siblings were not socially acceptable at school, but Fenton and Bridget were very close, and missed each other when they were apart for extended periods of time. Losing their mother had made the twins even more dependent on each other.

Fenton left his girlfriend Carlice and slid into the seat beside Bridget for first period. Carlice in her turn, sat beside Lena Lenore, gently pumping her for the latest gossip. Lena conveyed some of the more dramatic events in a sort of code, as Carlice was one of her best friends and privy to the group secrets.

"Is everything alright?" Fenton whispered.

"I think it is now," Bridget said. "I will tell you later."

Second period, Fenton continued sitting with Bridget and Carlice remained with Lena Lenore. Lena's boyfriend Eduard gave her a protective look, but continued to sit with one of the guys to allow the girls their bonding time.

Recess time, Bridget passed Jamie Lenore in the corridor and greeted him warmly. She noticed with a sense of dejavu that he was still talking with a wheeze. Jamie passed her concerns off casually.

"Either I really did have laryngitis, or Lena still has not forgiven me," Jamie whispered. "After all she went through yesterday - I didn't want to push her."

"I understand," Bridget whispered.

Although Lena had experienced a catharsis of her grief the previous day talking to her zombie parents, she might well harbor deep resentment that Jamie's parents were the ones who had survived. This illogical feeling could persist despite her uncle and aunt being so kind as to take Lena into their house, and treat her virtually as their own daughter. Lena's outlook on life was inclined to be pessimistic.

The rest of the school day flew, and after school Bridget got Fenton, who already had his driver's license and often had the use of the family car when Captain Etheridge drove his army issue jeep, to drop her off at the animal shelter. There she greeted Jenny Lenore, who was looking mildly shaken, but much like herself.

"Hi Jenny," Bridget called.

"Oh hello Bridget," Jenny called. "Are you here to take Biggs for a walk?"

"Yes," Bridget replied.

Jenny looked momentarily vague. "You were here yesterday - weren't you - when I collapsed?"

"Yes Jenny," Bridget replied. In her experience, most adults had to rationalize the mysterious events around the town in order to stay sane. Jenny Lenore lived near the edge of awareness, but she still denied full knowledge.

"I don't get migraine headaches very often," Jenny said. "But when I do - I get terrible hallucinations with them. I almost thought I spoke to Lena's parents yesterday."

"Imagine that," Bridget responded dryly.

"And wasn't there some silly talk among you kids about a wishing bowl?" Jenny said.

"It was just one of Great-Grandma Booth's antiques," Bridget said comfortably.

Jenny looked relieved. "That's what I thought!" she said.

Bridget continued her way around the back and collected Biggs. She secured him on his lease and led him out onto the street. Somehow Bridget was not surprised when Biggs put his nose to the ground and began leading Bridget in the direction of the high school. Mystic Evermore was a small town and everything was pretty much within walking distance.

When Bridget reached the school, Javier and Jeroma were sitting on the benches surrounding the oval watching the end of football practice. The Tilton's often stayed to watch Jaylen practice his football, and car pooled home with him later as they were almost related by marriage. Ivy Pinkerton had recently joined the spectators as Jaylen's official girlfriend.

Biggs ran up to Javier and sniffed him. "Hey boy," Javier said, and patted him on the head. "Was everything okay after I left yesterday Bridget?"

"Yeah - I had the Sheriff for company," Bridget said. "Although apparently she doesn't want Damien told that!"

"Adults!" Javier exclaimed. "Sometimes I'm sorry I'm on the verge of becoming one!"

"They do seem to lose the ability to deal with the truth in a straightforward manner," Ivy observed.

"Maybe we could practice, starting right now," Jeroma said. "What secrets are you two harboring?"

"Which ones would you like?" Javier said.

"The events of yesterday please," Jeroma said. "What's the use of being your little sis when I don't hear all your adventures?"

"Well there was a silver wishing bowl at the Lenore house if you believe in such things," Bridget began.

"I do," Jeroma said. She was rapt.

"I've been learning that anything can happen around here," Ivy agreed.

"And some of us accidentally made wishes that went wrong," Bridget continued. There were elements of the story she did not enjoy repeating, but Jeroma pressed her until she had told the whole tale.

"So now that you and Damien are definitely over - are you and Javier going to become an item?" Jeroma asked cheekily at the conclusion.

Bridget flushed. "I honestly don't know Jeroma."

Bridget peered shyly out from under her eyelashes at Javier. She had been propelled towards Damien by the intensity of her first teenage crush, but with Javier, there was a slower growing realization that he was an all-round nice person. Moreover, Damien had been an experienced man, ready to sweep Bridget off her feet. Despite his big-city background and Gothic interests, there was an inexperienced awkwardness about Javier.

Just then the football landed near them with a thump, and a group of boys ran up and grappled with one another over it. Biggs jumped and shrank against Javier.

"He is still nervous," Bridget observed. "I am supposed to be getting him used to the town and noises gradually."

"The puppy is much better around me," Javier said. "Perhaps I could help you walk him back to the shelter."

"That would be helpful," Bridget admitted.

"Jeroma - you will be alright going home with Jaylen won't you?" Javier inquired.

"Of course," Jeroma smiled.

"I will take care of her as well," Ivy promised.

Javier hauled himself to his feet and dusted off his black coat. He was very fastidious about his appearance. "Let's go Bridget," he said. "Here Biggs - walky!"

Biggs set off along the street looking pleased with himself. It was almost as though he had gone to collect Javier on purpose for this walk. They wound their way through the side streets until they reached the animal shelter.

"We drop Biggs off here," Bridget murmured.

The large gate was open as it was still business hours and they circled around the building without passing though reception. It was not necessary as Bridget was simply returning Biggs to his enclosure. After Bridget had settled Biggs down and given him a bowl of water, Javier asked to be shown through the animal shelter.

"I can sense that Jenny does a good thing here," Javier whispered. "Some of the new pets, down the back are sending out anxious and uncomfortable vibes, but the other pets appear to feel they are much happier and healthier than when they arrived."

"That is wonderful," Bridget murmured. "I wish I could communicate with the animals like you do."

"You are doing very well," Javier said. "In your own way."

"Let me show you my favorites," Bridget said and led the way into the cat section. She stopped in front of the cage housing Tiger and Tomson. "I had been hoping that a nice family would take these two," she whispered. "It worries me that they are still here."

"Why?" Javier asked in surprise.

"There is an awful woman, Mrs. Grey, who takes a lot of pets," Bridget confided. "She is not too bad with the dogs, but cats do not live very well with her. She doesn't bring them inside or give them any attention. It's nothing Jenny can have her charged with - but I want better for Tomson and Tiger."

"I see," Javier was thoughtful. "It is at times like this that my powers become a temptation."

"What do you mean?" Bridget exclaimed.

"I can't do a glamour or compulsion like a vampire and expect it to last," Javier said. "But I might be able to reduce Mrs. Grey's interest in acquiring new pets ever so slightly, by working with emotions she already has."

"Well you may be in luck, because I think I hear her voice now," Bridget whispered. "Mrs. Grey often comes late in the afternoon to see what animals have been released from quarantine that day."

"Ah there you are Bridget!" Mrs. Grey exclaimed. "Jenny told me to come out the back and look around."

Bridget hastily stepped away from the cage housing Tomson and Tiger as Mrs. Grey approached. She hovered in front of the cage housing an older female cat that had been in need of an adoptive home for some time.

"I'm not actually on duty today Mrs. Grey," Bridget said. "I have just been walking one of the puppies."

"Oh that's alright," Mrs. Grey exclaimed. "You know, with everything going on around here - I don't think I have seen any pets yet this week."

"It's only Tuesday, Mrs. Grey," Javier murmured politely.

Mrs. Grey turned her attention towards the wolf-whisperer. "Are you a new member of the staff?" she asked.

"I would like you to meet my friend Javier Tilton," Bridget explained.

"Nice to meet you Javier," Mrs. Grey responded. She peered into the closest cage. "What cat is this?"

"This is Marmalade," Bridget said. "She is a mature female looking for a home."

Mrs. Grey shrugged. "I think I have seen her before," she muttered. The middle-aged woman pushed her way past Bridget. "These two look lovely." She was pointing directly at Tomson and Tiger.

Bridget's heart went cold, but she felt powerless to say anything. Javier stepped into the breach.

"Were you happy with the pet you acquired last week?" Javier asked.

"Oh yes," Mrs. Grey gushed, momentarily distracted. She launched into a lengthy description of the antics of the puppy she had collected from the animal shelter most recently.

"We are very glad that you are pleased with the puppy," Javier reflected. "Are you really sure you want a pet today?"

Mrs. Grey shook her head. "I like to look," she said. "And when I have enough dogs, I like to get cats. They require so much less attention."

"I hope you enjoy looking around," Javier said. "And then, think what fun you can have with the puppy you took home last time!"

Javier gallantly led Mrs. Grey along the rows of cages, then out of the cat compound, and into the dog compound. Bridget was worried that at any minute, Mrs. Grey would turn around and demand Tomson or Tiger. If Bridget had attempted to distract the woman, she was sure her own powers of persuasion would have failed. However, Javier gave Mrs. Grey the full tour and then led her out past the reception area. Then he returned to Bridget.

"She didn't really want another pet," Javier said. "She would have taken one, however, if I had not given her that nudge towards her true feelings. I convinced her to be happier with what she already had, and to love her animals more deeply."

"I think you are amazing," Bridget said. She was flushed with excitement and gratitude and caught hold of Javier boisterously, sliding her hands inside his coat and around his body. Standing on tiptoe, she backed Javier up against the cage bars and kissed him passionately on the mouth. Javier was surprised, but returned Bridget's kiss clumsily. Tomson and Tiger reached through the bars of their cage and pulled at Javier's blonde hair.

After a moment or two, Bridget began to feel shy. She drew back from the kiss, but did not let go of Javier's waist. "You are warm," she whispered.

"Yeah, unlike HE whose name is not to be mentioned anymore," whispered Javier.

"Thank you so much for saving Tiger and Tomson," Bridget whispered, glad that they were still alone in the cat area.

"Speaking of Tomson and Tiger," Javier whispered, "They are pulling my hair."

"Sorry," Bridget whispered and stepped back from the cage, pulling Javier towards her.

"Bridget," Javier whispered seriously, "That was my first ever real kiss. I know I'm from the city - but honestly - I left Chicago before asking any girls out down there."

"I can tell," Bridget said. "You need some practice, but it's sorta cute."

Bridget was about to dive in for a second kiss, when they heard voices approaching the cat cages. It sounded like a father, mother and one or two children. They were out looking for their first ever family pet - a baby animal that would grow up with the child and be his constant companion whenever he was not at school.

Bridget and Javier broke apart, and Bridget hurried to greet the family. She inquired whether they were looking for a kitten or puppy. The mother replied that they were open to either, but felt that a cat might suit their family just a little better. When the boy was introduced to Tomson, he took a liking to the kitten immediately and stretched a hand out towards the bars.

Tomson sniffed the little boy's fingers and appeared attracted to his new owner. The family had not been looking for two cats, so Tomson and Tiger would be separated, but it had been too much to hope they could be kept together all their lives. The father went inside to organize the adoption with Jenny Lenore, while the mother and son remained with Bridget, getting to know the cat and talking about its care.

When the kitten had been packed into a cat carrier and the family had taken him home, Bridget turned to Javier with a questioning look upon her face. Javier shook his head.

"No I didn't influence them," Javier explained. "I never would!"

"Why not?" Bridget was curious.

"Because, if I had made them want to take the kitten, and then my influence wore off at home - they might have proven to be poor owners," Javier said. "The family had to want Tomson all by themselves to be committed owners."

"I see," Bridget mused. "Committed owners are always best for the animals."

"On the other hand," Javier said, "If my meddling with Mrs. Grey wears off and she becomes all emotionally needy again - she will simply return to her previous behavior. I haven't caused any harm."

Bridget looked slightly alarmed. "If Mrs. Grey comes back she might take Tiger!"

"I gave her a good push," Javier said. "I don't think she will be back to her old ways soon."

Bridget was petting Tiger through the bars. She stroked his ginger fur and outlined a few darker stripes. He was a tabby, with medium length fur and a friendly disposition. Tomson had been similar, but with a few endearing creamy patches.

"He is adorable," Bridget mused. "And with all our moving around - I've never had a pet of my own."

"I tell you what," Javier said. "If your father gives his permission, I will buy Tiger for you."

"Oh would you really?" Bridget was thrilled.

"Yes I would," Javier said, looking at the purring bundle of fur. "Unless you would prefer Biggs?"

"No," Bridget said. "I'm fond of Biggs, but I'm really helping him get over his nervousness so he can find his forever home. It is Tiger I would want."

"Well, Chicago wasn't a great place for pets either," Javier said. "So I wouldn't mind sharing the kitten with you, although I think we will agree he lives at your place. A new kitten might trip Grandpa Noah up at my place, although my Grandfather is wonderful for his age."

Bridget sent a hasty text message to Captain Etheridge and received the reply that he expected the placement at Mystic Evermore to last some time. The Agrarian Council had requested his on-going presence and the army was sensitive to the fact that he had lost his wife somewhat in the line of duty. Therefore a pet might be possible, whereas at previous places pets had not been advisable. Bridget scanned through the jumbled and somewhat equivocal message eagerly.

"So can I adopt a kitten?" Bridget asked in order to obtain a clearer answer.

"Yes," Captain Etheridge replied via text.

Bridget squealed in delight, and Javier went to speak to Jenny Lenore in reception, and organize the financial side of the adoption. A small fee had to be paid to cover vaccination, neutering and other veterinary services Tiger had received while at the shelter, and Bridget was advised to purchase a proper cat carrier. She also viewed a cuddly pet bed, but Jenny said that a cardboard box lined with an old blanket would be almost as comfortable for young Tiger.

The deposit paid, Bridget signed the ownership papers and entered Tiger's name onto a list that would ensure she was called if he ever got lost. Bridget and Javier debated gently carrying the cat carrier between them as they walked all the way to the Etheridge house, but in the end, Bridget called her brother Fenton and asked him to pick her up from the shelter.

Fenton was a little surprised to receive the call, which interrupted his romantic afternoon doing 'homework' at Carlice Favor's house; but was almost as excited as Bridget to hear they were allowed to have a pet. He arrived in the car and was introduced to Tiger, and then more subtly inducted into Javier's new status as Tiger's benefactor and special friend to Bridget.

Javier checked his watch and sighed. "Jeroma will be home by now," he said. "And while my parents are pretty lenient towards me, I had better be off too."

Javier refused Fenton's offer of a lift, because he said that his house was very central to Mystic Evermore, being just opposite the Woodgate house in the posh area. He gave Tiger one last pat and promised to visit him at the Etheridge house sometime. Then he faced Bridget.

"I will text you later if I may," Javier looked bashful despite, or perhaps because of, their shared kisses.

"I will look forward to it," Bridget said firmly. "And thank you so much for Tiger and everything."

"You are welcome," Javier said, and then strode off into the twilight with his long black woolen coat swirling around him. He walked upright and appeared as little afraid of the gathering dark as Damian Nevermore always had. Bridget supposed that when you could calm and tame most creatures, there was little to fear from being out of doors, even in an area like Mystic Evermore.

"Dad will be thrilled," Fenton remarked with a grin when they were alone in the car. "You have gone from a boyfriend who could tear your throat out - to one that has landed you with a kitten already."

"I don't think we are ready for the big introduction quite yet," Bridget said. "Technically - we haven't even begun dating yet."

"It will happen," Fenton predicted. "There is one bundle of fur in the back seat that guarantees it!"

"I look forward to it," Bridget whispered. "There is more to Javier than meets the casual eye."

****

PARABLE EIGHT: HALLOWEEN SPECIAL

My friend Carlice always seemed to be so confident and controlled. The perfect school girl, an A-list student and ideal girlfriend for my brother. While I knew that she was a vampire, I thought she had accepted her fate long ago. I had no idea how much she was still hurting inside.

(Bridget Etheridge's Journal)

Carlice Favor and her boyfriend Fenton Etheridge had a fight. Surprisingly, the fight was about the little ginger kitten that Javier Tilton had bought for Fenton's sister Bridget. Carlice had always adored cats, but Tiger was reluctant to sit on her lap. The baby animal had good instincts, and it sensed that Carlice was something unnatural - a vampire in fact.

Carlice had taken the kitten's aversion in her stride at first, as many things had been different since the accident that had transformed her into a vampire. Her diet for instance, while she could still eat human food for appearances' sake, only fresh lambs' blood formed a satisfactory substitute for the natural vampire diet of human blood.

The kitten was adorable, a bundle of ginger and white, medium fluffy tabby fur. At first Carlice was content to admire it squirming in Bridget's hands and running across the floor after its mistress when she served its food. However, after a while Carlice absolutely longed to touch the baby cat.

The first time Carlice reached out to the kitten, it turned away. It was occupied with a ball of wool at the time, so Carlice did not take the incident too seriously. However, the second time she approached, with a gentle tread and making all the right reassuring noises, the little kitten arched it's back, hissed and spat.

Fenton laughed, but Carlice was cut to the quick. "It is not funny," she cried.

"You will have to give it some time Carlice," Fenton said. "We knew this might be an issue."

"I have given Tiger time," Carlice replied glumly. "I've been visiting a few times - he ought to know me by sight now."

"Patience was never your greatest virtue," Fenton said, half meaning to be sympathetic, but sounding slightly critical.

"I know," Carlice sighed. She had other strengths: confidence, assertion, decisiveness, organization, energy and drive. These qualities usually brought her success. "It's just hard to be rejected by pet animals."

"Birds and bats still seem to like you," Fenton quipped. His attempt at humor was ill timed, however.

"That would be a great help if I wanted to be seen as a freak," Carlice retorted. She burst into tears.

Fenton approached to comfort his girlfriend and apologize for his thoughtless remarks. However, Carlice dodged him using her supernatural speed and ran out of the room. She opened the front door and burst into the garden. Fenton followed her as fast as he humanly could.

"At least let me give you a lift home," Fenton cried, his protective instincts stung. "It is getting dark outside.

"I don't need your protection," Carlice cried, which was true, but not very nice. As a vampire, Carlice was stronger and faster than most creatures on the streets of a sleepy country village at night. She had nothing to fear from a human assailant, and little to fear from a single unnatural predator either.

Carlice ran all the way home, which after all, was merely a couple of streets. Her Mother, Sheriff Sarah Favor looked up in surprise as Carlice slammed into the house.

"You are home early," Sarah Favor exclaimed. "I thought you would be with Fenton all evening, even though it is a school night!"

The Sheriff was surrounded by paperwork. Since she had the assistance of lead vampire Damien Nevermore in solving her cases, she had a good resolution rate. The reports were somewhat more challenging however, as unnatural perpetrators had to be explained in plausible terms to her human administration; and a high rate of deaths in custody also needed to be justified.

"We had a fight," Carlice cried. She crossed to the refrigerator and opened the door, taking out a box of crème filled chocolates to sweeten her mood. "I will be in my room the rest of the evening."

"What will you do?" the Sheriff asked curiously.

Carlice shrugged. "Watch TV, read a book, I suppose," she said. "I'm just not going to answer the telephone to Fenton Etheridge. Please don't let him inside."

"Let me know if you need anything dear," Sarah Favor said, returning her attention to her paperwork. If she were honest, the Sheriff would admit she was pleased to see her eighteen year old daughter acting so much like a normal teenage girl.

Carlice had always been difficult in a bright and beautiful sort of way. She had been diagnosed mildly obsessive-compulsive and could not bear to have one hair out of place, or be seen without a full face of make-up. She was the school beauty, and although she would never have admitted it at the time, also the school bitch.

Carlice was also a slave to the latest fashion. Sheriff Favor could not afford to indulge all of her daughter's clothing desires on the modest wage of a county Sheriff. However, Carlices' absentee father regularly sent packages of beautifully selected clothing back from the big city where he had moved to enjoy life with a new partner.

It had been a major shock when Sheriff Sarah Favor had discovered that Carlice had become a vampire. Carlice had hoped that her mother, who was quite rigid in her moral thinking, would never have to find out. However, Sheriff Sarah Favor belonged to the Agrarian Council, which aside from being a normal town council, was dedicated to fighting rogue vampires. The Sheriff therefore knew all the signs and symptoms of vampirism.

Sarah Favor had been in a particularly savage mood at the time, following the discovery that her new boyfriend and presumed toy-boy, Damien Nevermore, was actually a hundred year old vampire returned to town after an extended sabbatical elsewhere. The Sheriff had felt used and betrayed at this discovery, and her rage knew no bounds.

She had not staked Damien, possibly because he was related to the fabled Blackermores, whom the Agrarians allowed to remain in Mystic Evermore, because their presence discouraged supernatural immigration. Sarah Favor had instead broken up with Damien Nevermore with bitter words, and refused to see him for several months.

The Sheriff's reaction to the revelation that her daughter had become a vampire had also been fierce, and she had thrown Carlice out of the house for a week or two. Carlice had been shattered, and of necessity, retreated to Nevermore Manor, under the protection of Damien Nevermore. This circumstance made Carlice perceive Damien as some sort of weird older-brother-come-step-father, with whom she did not always see eye to eye.

When Sarah Favor had finally accepted her daughter back into her house, she had taken the precaution of sending her younger child, Kier, to live with his father. It had broken Sarah Favor's heart to have to choose between her two children, but her daughter clearly still needed her, and the Sheriff could not risk the 'infection' being spread to her beloved son. Carlice of course, missed her brother acutely.

Carlice reached her room and the Sheriff heard the door slam shut behind her daughter. A few minutes later, Fenton Etheridge drove up in the Etheridge family car. Fenton was a nice young man, who was always considerate. He also not afraid to face his girlfriend's mother even though she was the county Sheriff. Sarah Favor left her desk with a sigh and went out to the front door to greet him.

"She left her jacket behind," Fenton said.

"Thank you," Sheriff Favor accepted the jacket and put it down on a nearby chair. She did not invite Fenton to sit. "What was the fight about?"

Fenton looked puzzled. "I was tactless I think, but really I do not know," he admitted.

"I'm sorry I cannot let you speak to her at the moment," the Sheriff said.

"I will be on my mobile when Carlice has calmed down," Fenton promised faithfully.

Fenton was a genuine, straightforward sort of guy. He was also the son of Captain Etheridge, the special operations army captain who had been sent to Mystic Evermore to research a cure for vampirism. The couple hoped that one day, Carlice might become human again, so they could marry and have children. He climbed back into the vehicle and left.

Carlice had once been head cheer-leader; and dated the captain of the football team, Jaylen Woodgate. Her relationship with Jaylen Woodgate had collapsed, because Jaylen was struggling with the 'Woodgate curse'. Prior to coming into the 'Woodgate curse', which saw him transform into a werewolf once a month when the moon was full, Jaylen had been very chauvinistic. He had treated Carlice in a patronizing and sexist manner and their relationship had bordered on the toxic. Sarah Favor reflected that Fenton was a great improvement.

Upstairs, Carlice had thrown herself down onto her bed in a fit of sobbing. Such tempestuous behavior was unusual for the blonde beauty. After her transformation into a vampire, Carlice had channeled all of her will power into regaining the control required to live like a normal senior high school girl. Within a few weeks, Carlice had returned to her place as social leader at the high school.

The next arrival at the Favor house was Damien Nevermore. Over the past weeks, the Sheriff's feelings towards Damien Nevermore had changed considerably. Trust had developed and she was pleased to see him. Sarah was waiting for the right moment to tell Damien that more tender feelings had developed, and see whether the hundred year old vampire who could possibly live forever, would consider anything like a permanent relationship with a mere mortal and mother of two.

"Hello Damien," Sarah Favor said, opening the front door once again. This time she invited the visitor inside. "Come in and sit down."

Damien was bearing gifts. He had an apple pie, and bottle of fine red wine. The box of chocolates that Carlice was even now gorging, had also been a gift from Damien. Sarah Favor appreciated Damien's attention to the niceties of courtship - if indeed that was what was going on between the two of them.

"I thought you might like to take a break and enjoy a little snack," Damien suggested.

The Sheriff giggled and blushed at the thought of where a bottle of red wine consumed in the evening might lead. "Unfortunately," she admitted. "Carlice is at home. She and Fenton had a fight."

Damien looked concerned. "Is she alright?" he asked.

"I don't know," Sarah Favor said. "I haven't wanted to invade her privacy. A girl doesn't want her mother always interfering!"

"We will go and talk to her together," Damien suggested.

Damien was possibly the only person in Mystic Evermore who would dare disturb a sulking Carlice in her bedroom. With the disappearance of the Blackermores, who had traditionally kept order in the lich community, Damien Nevermore had inherited their mantle as lead vampire. This inheritance had effectively transformed him from aging dilettante into kind shepherd.

"Sure," Sarah agreed. Bursting into her daughter's bedroom accompanied by Damien was a far different thing, than presuming to enter alone.

Damien and Sarah mounted the stairs and knocked on Carlice's bedroom door.

"Damien is here," Sarah called.

There was a short scuffle and Carlice's door opened a crack. "Thanks for the chocolates Damien," Carlice said.

"They were for your mother," Damien observed.

"I need them more," Carlice replied. "Besides, I'm saving Mum from putting on weight."

"Very true," Sarah agreed.

"What is wrong?" Damien said.

"Fight with Fenton," Carlice admitted.

Damien and Sarah already knew that, so Sarah tried another tack: "Tomorrow is Halloween," she said. "I have organized for my deputy to be on duty so we could dress up and hand out candy to the trick and treaters."

This was a considerable concession, which Carlice recognized immediately. Halloween was often a busy evening for the county police, with practical jokes gone wrong to cause injury, and the occasional real crime camouflaged by all the excitement and activity. Sarah Favor had often been lax in her parenting duties, due to dedication towards her policing duties, leaving Carlice to go trick and treating with either the Woodgates or the Lenores.

"I appreciate that Mum," Carlice sobbed. "But the fun has sorta gone out of Halloween since I woke up as the monster!"

Damien chortled: "That is a statement worthy of me at my most cynical," he observed.

"It's been about a year now," Carlice cried. "At first, I responded to the challenge of regaining control. Now I'm tired of being different."

"Let me talk to her alone," Damien suggested.

Sarah Favor nodded and returned to her paperwork in the study. She helped herself to a slice of the apple pie and brewed a strong cup of coffee to keep herself going. She knew Damien would not mind. He did not really eat human food. Nor did Carlice, although she still seemed to retain a sweet tooth and like chocolates.

Damien followed Carlice into the bedroom and sat down on the opposite side of the room. He had been changed into a vampire when he was around twenty years of age, and his handsome good looks made him appear suited to dating the daughter; but they both knew that his one hundred plus years of experience inclined him towards the sophisticated company of the mother.

"Tell me about your transformation," Damien invited. "It was around about the time I came to town wasn't it?"

Carlice nodded. "A little after," she said. "I went to the hospital for an emergency appendectomy. A routine procedure really. They tell me that I had some sort of unprecedented allergic reaction... causing internal bleeding."

"I see," Damien murmured. "I had heard something of the sort..."

"Well," Carlice continued. "The Doctor recommended a blood transfusion, and I don't know how it happened - but the bag was full of vampire blood."

Carlice looked at Damien expectantly, but he shook his head. "I'm afraid it wasn't mine," he said. "I was busy stealing blood from the hospital and the butcher, not donating it..."

"And Eduard?" Carlice inquired.

"He was trying to fit in at the school, but I'm pretty sure he did not donate blood," Damien said. "Neither of us was your sire."

"But who does that leave?" Carlice demanded.

"A rogue vampire or one of the Blackermores," Damien concluded. "We know you fell ill when the Mater Vampire was killed... so that would point to you being one of the Blackermore bloodline."

"Why would they do such a thing?" Carlice cried.

Damien looked thoughtful. "Perhaps they were recruiting through the hospital."

Carlice looked horrified. "Why would they do such a thing?"

Damien sighed. "I think I have explained before. The Blackermores' weren't really good or bad. They were simply peace loving and neutral. Unlike you and me - they viewed the change as a gift. If they donated blood to the hospital, it would only have changed someone who died of natural causes."

Carlice shuddered. "So I actually died?"

"I expect so," Damien said. "You said you had a severe allergic reaction. Perhaps your heart gave out at one point."

"I don't know," Carlice murmured. "I don't remember. I just know I woke with this messy urge to snack on my friends' throats." She shuddered. "It was a nightmare... but it would not go away. I forced it - but I still had to drink some sort of blood."

"I've been through it too," Damien said. "And I did not regain control nearly as quickly as you... in fact, it took me twenty odd years."

"I've never killed a person," Carlice murmured. "A few people have even said I'm 'nicer' since the change, because I'm less of a tyrant and more understanding towards my friends. I even talk to the less popular kids... and I've met Fenton, who accepts me the way I am."

"It is ironic isn't it?" Damien muttered. "We don't know the joy of living until we have lost it..."

"I will think about the Halloween thing," Carlice said.

"You do that," Damien said. "It would mean a lot to your mother."

"Wil you come along?" Carlice asked.

"If you two will have me," Damien said. "And if the unnatural community stays peaceful during the festival."

It was Damien's turn to sigh. He had inherited a lot of responsibility with the disappearance of the Blackermores.

"Perhaps you could put Eduard in charge for the evening," Carlice suggested.

Damien's younger brother Eduard was in Carlices' senior class at Mystic Evermore High. Eduard was also a hundred year old vampire, but he masqueraded as a normal school boy.

Damien shook his head. "Not Eduard, besides, he wants to spend the evening with Lena."

"Christopher then," Carlice suggested.

"Christopher does make a good second-in-command," Damien admitted. "He is amazingly loyal. And I will swear that at times, he almost channels Rachel Blackermore. It must be all the hours he spends adoring her statue."

"It's a pity we can't get her back for him," Carlice suggested.

"I can't," Damien said. "I've spent some hours researching vampire lore, but I've found nothing."

"What about the witches?" Carlice suggested.

"Raven, Paul and John?" Damien mused. "It's an idea. I could ask them as a favor. Now that Paul is coming into his powers, and John has regained the stolen Booth powers, they might be able to achieve even the impossible."

Carlice giggled: "If it were possible by natural means, it would not be magic."

"Captain Etheridge might not agree with you there," Damien observed. "He has been achieving the unexpected by means of science."

Carlice sobered a little at the mention of her boyfriend's father. "I guess I ought to talk to Fenton," she said. "He meant no harm really."

"I will go downstairs and see whether your mother is missing me," Damien said.

"She won't be," Carlice laughed. "She has far too much paperwork."

"She might like a shoulder massage," Damien's eyes gleamed wickedly and his fangs showed slightly.

'You wicked, wicked man," Carlice cried in mock anger. "You came here to seduce my mother."

"No such crude thing," Damien objected. "Not unless Sarah wants it."

"Knowing my Mother, there will be strings attached," Carlice warned.

Damien laughed. "That is part of Sarah's charm," he replied.

****

You would think that the Education Department would make Halloween a school holiday, for all the excitement it involves! The students were fidgety all day, and a few managed to sneak out early, with notes from their parents of course. Carlice was one of the lucky ones, as Sheriff Favor had decided she wanted to spend the afternoon shopping with her daughter.

After the shopping was completed, Carlice and Sarah Favor set to work cooking sweets for that evening. Carlice found that preparing to celebrate Halloween with her mother was fun, and wished that they had done so more often. She really appreciated the Sheriff making the time to spend with her daughter, and they spent the afternoon making popping candy and brownie slices to hand out at the door.

Carlice supposed that as a mature eighteen year old, she was too old to join the trick and treaters who would troop from house to house, although her friend Lena Lenore and a few other seniors were tagging along with the juniors. Their excuse was that it would be their last year, until they joined the procession of parents and chaperones who hovered around to ensure everyone's safety.

A smashing witch costume had arrived in the mail from her father, although this made her mother look wistful, as most contact with her unrepentant paternal parent did. Sarah Favor wore one of the costumes her daughter had worn on a previous year. It was a 'good witch' costume, and its voluminous skirts and bodice lacing allowed it to be adjusted to her mother's more mature figure.

Damien Nevermore did not end up joining the Favor household Halloween celebration as had been discussed. The lead vampire had heard a rumor of a skirmish up around the South Carolina border, so together with fellow vampire Christopher, and the hunter Jamie Lenore, he was off to check it out.

Raven Booth, Jamie Lenore's girlfriend, was once again angry that Jamie accompanied Damien on a mission that could prove dangerous, but the adventurous youth could not be restrained, arguing that his peaceful residence in Mystic Evermore contradicted his natural inclinations. There were some arguments that even a Hudu practitioner could not win.

When Carlice and her mother had finished cooking Halloween candy, they cleaned up the kitchen, and then set to decorating the house. They hung an ugly artificial spider over the doorframe and festooned the surrounding area with toilet paper woven to represent a hanging web. Then Carlice ran down the drive-way to decorate the front gate with black and orange bows. She wasn't quite sure what they represented, but she thought they looked cool and would guide trick and treaters up to the house.

Sarah Favor hung a shiny orange backdrop printed with black cats and other Halloween motifs, across the hallway so no one could see into the rest of the house. Instead they would see the spooky alcove where Carlice and Sarah would be standing to give out candy. They had purchased several battery operated pumpkins, which would glow and throw a dim light after dark.

It was still twilight when the first wave of trick and treaters arrived. They were younger children, whose parents would want to put them to bed at a reasonable hour. Most of them were accompanied by their guardians, a fact that the Sheriff viewed with approval as she was very safety conscious.

A number of children could not recognize the Sheriff in her good witch costume instead of her usual khaki uniform. This made their parents laugh, because usually the Sheriff was a distinctive figure in the community.

Sarah Favor blushed and was embarrassed at first, but then she too began to enjoy the joke. The children thanked their hostesses for the candy and moved on to the next house.

After the wave of young children, high school freshmen and juniors began to arrive. They recognized Carlice and snickered behind their hands at the Sheriff in her good witch costume. Luckily the Sheriff had got used to being laughed at by now, and giggled to see the teens covert attempts to disguise their laughter.

Sarah and Carlice had set up a large tub on the front verandah, where the youth could bob for apples. Carlice knelt down to encourage a couple of timid freshmen who were reluctant to get their faces wet. Thankful for the wonders of water-proof make-up, Carlice plunged her face deep into the bowl and bit at the closest apple. It bounced off her nose and floated away from her. The freshmen laughed.

Carlice hated to be beaten by anything, so she took a deep breath and plunged her head back into the tub. She allowed her fangs to extend slightly and sunk them securely into an apple, emerging triumphant. The she reached up and pulled the apple out of her mouth, not realizing that the fangs were still extended.

The freshmen stared at Carlice in wonder. "That was very clever," one of the girls exclaimed.

"But you do have funny teeth," another girl observed. "I've never seen any quite like them."

"You should get braces," a boy suggested. He grinned to show that he had a full mouth of metal himself.

"They are fake teeth, just for tonight," Carlice lied. She was shocked to think how close she had come to revealing her abnormality. Still, Halloween celebrations formed the perfect excuse. "Now that I have shown you what to do, you can get apples for yourselves."

Carlice scrambled to her feet and retreated to stand beside her mother.

Sarah Favor looked at her quizzically. "Is everything all right?" she asked.

Carlice nodded. "I just got a bit wet," she said.

"It is a cool evening," Sarah observed. "Perhaps you could use the hair dryer to dry off."

"Good thinking," Carlice agreed. "But what about the kids - they are getting wet?"

"They are also running around getting dry," the Sheriff observed. "We are standing still giving out candy. But now you mention it, maybe we ought to put a large towel out so they can dry off."

"Yes!" Carlice replied. She went inside and returned with a dark green towel. "An old one Dad left behind will do just fine."

As the evening progressed, a few seniors joined the trick and treaters. Anna Vaughn and Mike Davis arrived accompanied by their younger siblings Netta Davis and Nathan Vaughn. Anna Vaughn complimented the Sheriff on her use of electronic jack-o-lanterns, as they were "so much safer than candles". The Sheriff laughed and agreed because Anna's uncle, Ben Vaugh was with the fire department.

Carlice gently teased Anna about being seen out with Mike Davis once again. No one knew whether 'sensible' Anna, who was also school captain, and 'practical' Mike Davis, who steadfastly refused to acknowledge the fact that some of his friends were vampires, had commenced a relationship, or were 'just good friends' still. Possibly even Anna and Mike did not know yet.

Anna blushed: "Shut up, Carlice," she exclaimed. "Mike is just someone who agrees with me about stuff."

"That is very important," Sheriff Sarah Favor added, overhearing. "A relationship won't survive without some common ground."

"And he gets along with Nathan," Anna admitted.

Mike and Nathan were laughing together about some boy joke. "Come on Anna," Nathan called. "Don't stop to gossip at every house!"

"I'll see you at school," Anna added hurriedly and scuttled after her brother and male friend.

Power couple Eduard Nevermore and Lena Lenore appeared to be hanging out with Zarah Strahan and Paul Booth for the evening. Zarah and Paul were both juniors, and in the flush of their first romance. They were accompanied by Zarah's younger brother Benji Strahan, who was a brainy nerd and took a few junior classes despite being in his freshman year.

Benji Strahan reminded Carlice of her brother Keir, because he had once been Keir's best friend. Carlice was happy Keir got to see more of their father than she did, but she wished he still lived at home. She sometimes wondered whether her mother did too. Perhaps now that her mother understood Carlice's vampirism was not contagious, she might let Keir come home.

When the Strahans had left, Carlice turned to her mother. "I miss Keir," she said.

"So do I," Sarah Favor sighed. "Perhaps, if things work out with Damien, Keir could come home."

Carlice frowned. "I would love to have Keir home," she exclaimed. "But that doesn't make sense. You sent him away because there was one vampire in the house. Why would you call him back because there were two?"

"Damien would be a father figure," Sarah surmised. "That is important for a boy." Then the Sheriff blushed and shushed her daughter because more trick and treaters were approaching.

Javier Tilton and Bridget Etheridge were escorting Javier's younger sister Jeroma around town that evening. Javier always insisted that his name was said with a "J" instead of the Hispanic "H", so that his name matched his sister's. Bridget was full of blushes, because she and Javier were new to each other's company. They were well on the way to becoming a couple, but Bridget was far less self-possessed than when she had her crush on Damien Nevermore. In company with Javier, the red head appeared to be opening up and truly falling in love.

Carlice did not see her ex-boyfriend, Jaylen Woodgate and his new girlfriend, Ivy Pinkerton anywhere. This surprised Carlice somewhat, although glancing at the sky, she wondered whether the moon was full enough for Jaylen to have his own business - werewolf business - that evening.

Alternately, Ivy could be at home with her young step-brother Liam, father Sunny and young step-mother Estella. Ivy's grandmother, Old Lady Pinkerton, was well known as the town prude and might not approve of Halloween celebrations. Old Lady Pinkerton and her church cronies were the best cooks in the county and catered for most special events, so their peculiarities were tolerable most of the time.

Carlice and Sarah gave out candy until the stock they had made was exhausted. Carlice had thought she would miss being one of the trick or treaters, but she found it was even more exciting to wait in her prepared domain, allowing the costumes and excitement to come to her. It was also rare for her mother to take the time off to do something like celebrate Halloween with her daughter.

Towards the end of the evening, Fenton arrived to take Carlice to the after-party down at the Snack Bar. He was dressed in a black track-suit, and had horns on his head. He also carried a pitch fork. His skin was redder than his hair because he had liberally applied face paint.

"I guess you are meant to be a devil?" Carlice exclaimed.

"Well, I would be green if I was an alien - wouldn't I?" Fenton joked.

"Not necessarily," Carlice reflected. She kissed her mother on the cheek. "Thanks for doing the Halloween thing with me, Mum. I had the greatest time."

"I'm glad you enjoyed yourself," Sarah Favor replied. "Don't worry about cleaning up. What I haven't finished tonight - we can do tomorrow."

"Thanks, Mum," Carlice replied. A sudden thought struck her. "Would you like to come with us?"

"It's nice of you to ask," Sarah Favor said. "But I think I'll finish my evening by getting some sleep."

"Alright," Carlice ran into her bedroom and picked up her handbag. "I'm ready Fenton."

Sarah Favor began collecting together the used candy bowls on the sink for washing up. Then she began sweeping the foyer, which was littered with wrappers and dirty foot-prints from the multiple visitors to the house that evening. She was humming to herself happily and looked very young in the blue good witch costume. Young for the mother of an eighteen year old that was.

Fenton looked puzzled. "Whatever is up with your mother?" he whispered as they shut the door behind them and climbed down the short steps off the verandah.

"I think she hopes that Damien will return before the end of the evening," Carlice admitted. "But that is unlikely because Damien went off to South Carolina."

"I guess your mum can have her dreams," Fenton observed.

Carlice grimaced. "She was talking like we would all be living together earlier," she whispered.

Fenton whistled: "Would Damien move out to the Sheriff's house, or you and the Sheriff move into the Manor?"

"I don't think they would have a choice," Carlice said. "Nevermore Manor is more defensible for Damien's purposes."

"But Eduard lives there," Fenton objected. "And the Manor is full of secrets."

"Eduard could move into one of the cottages like Christopher did," Carlice said. "He and Lena are always looking for more privacy."

"This is all conjecture," Fenton said. "Damien told Bridget he was not the settling down type. It was the reason he gave for their break-up."

"Perhaps with my mother - it would be different," Carlice speculated.

Fenton had the family car, because his father had access to the army issue jeep, and Fenton's mother was deceased, so she would not be driving anywhere. Indeed, it was just a week until the three month anniversary of Mrs. Etheridge's death, something that the Etheridge twins were trying not to dwell upon.

"Speaking of Bridget," Fenton said as he started the vehicle. "We are meeting Bridget and Javier at the Snack Bar, I hope you don't mind."

"I love Didge," Carlice, who got on very well with Fenton's sister usually, exclaimed. "And it's so sweet to see her with Javier, she used to despise him as a fake."

"That was before Bridget realized Javier had something going on of his own," Fenton observed reasonably.

Fenton turned the car lights on. A dog was standing on the edge of the motorway looking at them in surprise. Its eyes glowed huge and round in the sudden light of the car. It was a medium sized canine, and large enough to be intimidating to the passer-by. Fenton tooted the horn. The dog was confused and remained frozen in the headlights. If he tried to drive, it would likely panic and run in the wrong direction.

"The poor thing," Carlice exclaimed. "We can't run it over. I will get out and shoo it away."

Carlice opened the passenger side door and approached the feline. She thought briefly about Bridget's kitten and how he would not let her pick him up. That did not seem to matter anymore, as the purpose of her errand was to save the creature from being run over.

"Go home," Carlice cried, waving her arms. "Good doggie."

Her voice appeared to break the spell holding the dog, and it turned and trotted down the footpath. About half-way down the street, it entered a neighbors' garden and seemed to settle on the porch. It was probably the household pet.

"People should tie their animals up on Halloween," Fenton observed as Carlice clambered back into the car. "There are so many strange lights and smells."

"It is not quite as bad as the fourth of July," Carlice added as she shut the car door. "Dogs really hate fireworks!"

"That was well done you know," Fenton observed as they took off. "Not everyone likes to approach a strange dog."

"I couldn't let it get hurt," Carlice said. She had a soft heart and adored domestic animals. That had not changed just because she had become a vampire.

****

Fenton and Carlice drew up at the Snack Bar after a few minutes, because in a small town like Mystic Evermore, nothing was very far away. The rear car park was full and for once it was difficult to find parking. Fenton ended up leaving the car out the front, some meters away from the shops.

"The whole town must be here tonight," he exclaimed.

"Cool," Carlice cried, and catching hold of Fenton's hand, skipped along beside him. There was nothing Carlice loved better than a major get-together.

Fenton and Carlice entered the Snack Bar and scanned the crowded dining area until they spied Javier and Bridget seated in one of the booths along the side. Jeroma was seated opposite them, but when she saw the seniors approaching, she slid out of the booth and fetched a spare chair from near the server.

Jeroma fidgeted on the edge of the chair and then announced she would be going to say, "Hello," to Zarah and Benji Strahan. Fenton and Carlice slid into the booth opposite Bridget and Javier.

"Did you have a good time trick and treating?" Carlice asked Bridget.

"I always have the best time with Javier," Bridget gushed.

Javier leaned closer to the red head and whispered into her ear. "I'm afraid I might have accidentally used my special voice on you," he admitted.

"That's all right," Bridget said. "It feels so good... you can use the voice with my permission." She rested back into the circle of Javier's arm with a blissful smile on her face.

"What is the difference between using the voice and a glamour?" Fenton inquired with a glance at Carlice.

"Well," Javier tried to explain. "A wolf-whisperer works with a person's natural inclinations. So - if I wanted to make someone forget they overheard this conversation - I would enhance their thought that it was very noisy in the Snack Bar and encourage them to believe what we said made no sense at all!"

"But I could take the conversation right out of their mind," Carlice admitted. "Although as Javier said - it is too noisy to be overheard clearly here. His method is better in my opinion."

"I'm going to order us some snacks," Fenton said to his girlfriend. "What would you like Carlice?"

Carlice perused the menu. "Well I spent the afternoon making candy and sampled a bit too much, so something savory," she said. "Hot-dog with the lot please."

Fenton stood up and moved over to the cashier to order. The queue was quite long so he would be away for a few minutes. Javier counted his pennies and offered to buy Bridget a second serving of her favorite ice-cream sundae. The girl accepted happily, and Javier followed Fenton to the server.

Bridget turned to Carlice for some girl-talk: "Fenton said you had some sort of argument yesterday - something to do with Tiger?"

"Everything is all right now," Carlice explained. "It wasn't important."

"It must have been something," Bridget persisted.

"Well," Carlice flushed. "Sometimes I miss the way things could have been... and the kitten would not come to me for a cuddle."

"I'm sorry," Bridget was quick to sympathize. She patted Carlice on the hand, barely noticing that the vampire's appendage was cooler than a normal human hand.

"If your father succeeds in finding a cure," Carlice murmured hopefully. "Things will be different."

Bridget frowned. "Do you think perhaps you count on that a little too much?" she asked. "Dad's cure is nowhere near ready - and may never be. Damien took it once - and it saved his life - but he is still Damien."

"I know what you mean," Carlice admitted.

"So what does the future hold for you and Fenton without?" Bridget persisted.

Carlice frowned. "College, jobs, travel..."

"I guess you could adopt," Bridget murmured.

"Anything is possible," Carlice murmured in return. "We will have to wait and see."

"You two are boring," Jeroma announced sliding back into her seat at the end of the booth. "Talking like grown-ups."

Jeroma Tilton was privy to some of the town secrets because she was Javier's younger sister. However, she did not know everything that went on, and Javier was determined to shelter her as much as possible. Bridget and Carlice respectfully changed the subject.

"Well - what have you been up to young Jeroma?" Carlice inquired.

"This and that," Jeroma replied. "Jaylen's football has been pretty exciting to watch... I like to swim at the recreation center my father manages... and I even got dragged along to Javier's baseball as a fielder."

Carlice looked surprised. "I didn't know that our baseball team was mixed," she exclaimed.

"I don't know if it is exactly," Bridget observed.

"Mystic Evermore baseball is more casual than competition," Jeroma explained. "Nothing like what it was back in Chicago."

"I thought you might be back if you smelled ice-cream," Javier said. He placed a plate in front of Jeroma. "I got you a scoop of each."

"Ooh, thanks," Jeroma exclaimed. She picked up her spoon.

"And here is your hot-dog," Fenton said to Carlice. "I got your special strawberry shake too. The counter staff looked at me funny until explained it was for you."

Carlice picked up her special shake and sipped it. The added lamb's blood rushed through her body and warmed her throughout. She curled her toes in pleasure. "You are the best boy-friend ever," she exclaimed, and gave Fenton a warm hug.

Just then the electric lights began to flicker. The next moment the Snack Bar was plunged into darkness, the only illumination coming from the pumpkin candles on the tables. Mike Davis, who worked at the Snack Bar on the weekends, raced out into the kitchen to check the fuse-box. He came back shaking his head.

"It's no good," Mike announced. "It is not the fuses."

The customers sitting nearest to the windows looked out into the street. Everything was dark outside as well. Instead of staying seated sensibly, a few people got up and started milling around.

"Don't panic," the Snack Bar Staff Member on duty urged. "Eat your food, and then if the lights are still out - go home quietly."

Some people obeyed them and sat back down.

"The street lights are out too!" Anna Vaughn cried.

"I bet it is a Halloween prank," Mike said loudly to anyone who was listening.

"This is why Mum rarely takes Halloween off," Carlice exclaimed.

"Well, my Dad will be onto it," Fenton replied. "My Dad and the deputies. They will find out who did it."

"My Uncle Ben and the Fire Department will be looking into it," Anna announced importantly. "If any electric lines are down there could be quite a lot of danger."

"I hope nobody crashed into an electric pole," remarked Lena Lenore, who had lost both her parents in a similar accident just over a year ago.

"I am sure it is nothing like that," observed Lena's boyfriend, Eduard Nevermore in a comforting tone.

"Can you see in the dark?" Bridget whispered to her boyfriend Javier.

"About the same as you I suppose," Javier replied. "I talk to animals, not look through their eyes."

"Oh," Bridget sounded vaguely disappointed. "But if there were an animal around?"

"I might be able to ask it what it saw," Javier admitted. He began to concentrate. "As far as I can tell - the lights are out all over Mystic Evermore. The owl I spoke to was not too concerned. He said nothing is out there."

"Yes, it's all very quiet," Carlice confirmed, reaching out with her super-sensitive vampire hearing. Her eyes were adjusting as well, although she was suffering some afterimages from the sudden failure of the electric lighting.

"Maybe too quiet," Eduard Nevermore suggested. He had steered Lena over to their table. Zarah, Paul and Benji had followed closely behind him.

"I have finished my ice-cream," Jeroma announced. "Please take me home Javier. If this is a joke, I don't think it is a funny one anymore."

"At least we would find out if the car lights were still working," Paul Booth said.

"Why would the car lights fail?" Javier sounded puzzled. "They aren't connected to the mains."

Paul gave an embarrassed cough. He glanced around to make sure no one else was listening, but Anna, Mike and the community customers had formed their own cluster. Paul grabbed Javier by the coat cuff and steered him and Bridget outside. Eduard and Lena followed, with Carlice and Fenton close behind. Zarah, Jeroma and Benji were a little slower.

"Between you and me - we have been having a lot of this sort of thing at home lately," Paul Booth admitted. "Since Dad took the stolen Booth powers into his body. After years of being relatively powerless, he wasn't prepared to control the sudden surge."

"How would he cause something like this?" Fenton asked curiously.

"He would think about how dark it was perhaps - or worry about not finding the light switch and his thought would become reality," Paul whispered.

"That doesn't make sense," Eduard said.

Paul shrugged. "It's magic."

"Or physics," Javier suggested. "Perception affects reality - like Schrodinger's cat!"

"Speculative physics in the extreme," Benji Strahan observed.

"Well, whatever it is, we have been suffering from it all week," Paul murmured.

"Why don't you just fix it?" Javier asked. "Aren't you a Booth witch too?"

Paul looked embarrassed in the moonlight. "Unfortunately, the powers Dad took in are stronger than mine - I can't override his spells."

Eduard crossed the car park to his car. He unlocked the door and reached into the cabin to flick the light switch. "No lights!" he exclaimed.

"So - it probably is my Dad," Paul said.

"What do we do?" Fenton asked.

"We could all drive in convoy to my house," Paul suggested. "Carefully of course, because there are no lights."

"Alright," Javier said. He climbed into his car and called Bridget and Jeroma to follow.

Javier nosed the vehicle carefully out of the parking space, before pulling aside and waited for Eduard to lead the way with Lena, Paul and Benji in the other car. Eduard had a vampire's ability to see in the dark, so he maneuvered his vehicle with confidence.

"Our car was out the front," Fenton exclaimed.

"I suggest you let me drive," Carlice said. "I have excellent night vision."

"Of course," Fenton fumbled to hand her the keys in the dark.

The three cars drove carefully one after the other through the darkened town. Eduard and Carlice had excellent night vision, but all Javier could do was stay close behind and follow their lead. The procession left the central business district, passed by the affluent streets and headed towards the poorer area, where the Booths resided. Luckily there were very few other cars on the road that evening.

Finally they pulled up in front of the Booth house, which was always neat and tidy because John Booth was an excellent handyman. The house was dark apart from the weak glow of candle light through the window of the front room.

Paul Booth jumped out of the car and led the way through the front door.

"Dad," he called. "Where are you?"

"In here, son," John's voice sounded from the modest lounge room. "I'm afraid I've done it again."

Paul felt his way into the lounge. Javier, Bridget and Jeroma followed closely. Zarah and Benji stuck close together, while Eduard, Lena and Carlice hung back.

John peered at the teens' faces in the candlelight. "You have brought some of your friends?" he asked Paul.

"Yes, Dad," Paul affirmed. "You know Zarah and Benji, Carlice is the Sheriff's daughter, Javier and Jeroma are Noah Bumble's grandchildren. The others are Bridget and Fenton Etheridge, Eduard Nevermore and his girlfriend Lena Lenore."

"It's nice to meet you," John Booth said. "And it's good to hear my son is making friends outside of his err, grade."

Carlice laughed. "My generation are beginning to reject the town social stratification," she said, stepping forward and proffering her hand to John Booth in the dark. "And I understand you now work for the Agrarian Council."

"I am their maintenance person," John Booth agreed proudly. He accepted Carlice's hand and held it gently. "I sense you have been changed?"

"Unfortunately yes," Carlice murmured. "Perhaps you heard about the incident at the hospital?"

"Many things happen at the hospital," John dismissed the idea. "And you generally get worse treatment if you are Black than white."

"That's so wrong," Benji Strahan muttered fiercely.

"Not all townsmen are as progressive as your father, Benji dear," John Booth murmured. Robbie Strahan, the town plumber, was unusual in his equalitarian stance, and he had even offered apprenticeships to John Booth's two sons. Wilson was well on his way to becoming a qualified plumber in his own right, but Paul was still at school.

"Back to the problem at hand," Paul said firmly. "You have taken the entire town lights out."

"That's not possible," John Booth exclaimed in alarm. "You know my 'accidents' are usually localized."

"Some people say a witch's powers are magnified on Halloween," Eduard suggested diplomatically.

John Booth scoffed. "Halloween is a lot of tin-kettling and nonsense," he asserted. "It's November 1, All Saints, that is powerful."

"With respect sir," Carlice persisted. "The town lights are all out!"

"Well," John Booth said thoughtfully. "I remember I was thinking I might have forgotten to pay the power bill and the electric lights might be cut off."

Paul Booth sighed. "The phrasing is very important. He thought 'electric lights' so even the head-lamps were affected."

"But the refrigerator is still cool," John said. "I checked."

"Luckily!" Paul exclaimed. "So a lot of essential services are still functioning. And we were able to start the cars..."

John Booth cradled his head in despair. "It's like having a loaded gun in my head," he began to moan.

"Don't finish that thought Dad," Paul said sharply. He made a hasty gesture, and his father froze, trapped in a moment of time.

"My oath," Carlice exclaimed. "I would have hated to see what happened if he had continued to say 'and it could go off at any time'."

Zarah and Bridget gasped in horror. "He could have splattered his brains," Bridget cried.

"Or hit one of us," Eduard observed wryly.

"Yeah, that's why I stopped him," Paul said.

"That would have been awful," Jeroma's eyes were wide.

"And like I said," Paul moaned, "I'm not generally powerful enough to countermand him."

"I might be able to help," Javier, who had hitherto been quietly thinking, offered.

Paul looked at him in surprise. "You are not even a witch!"

"Wolf-whisperer," Javier said. "If I can convince your father that he is able to control these new powers... the danger would go away."

"Do you think you could really do that?" Paul asked.

"He sent Andrew Jackson to sleep," Carlice observed. "And Jackson is a vampire aristocrat."

Paul looked alarmed. "Well don't send Dad to sleep - if he had a nightmare..."

"I understand," Javier said. "I would proceed very carefully."

"The first thing is to stop him blowing his brains out when he unfreezes," Eduard advised.

"Well for that, I suggest you put him in the shower, fully clothed, with the water running," Javier said.

"Why?" Bridget was amazed.

"Hopefully the shock will stop him completing his thought," Javier said.

"It's worth a try," Paul said. He turned to Eduard, "Help me carry him please."

Paul and the strong young vampire easily carried John Booth into the shower, where they propped him up against the wall. Paul turned the water on, and Eduard continued to steady the older man. Paul made a gesture and time began to flow around his father once again.

"What the?" John Booth spluttered. "How did I get here?"

"You were thinking bad thoughts sir," Javier said in a soothing voice. "Please don't try to remember them."

"Alright," John Booth said, stepping out of the shower alcove and turning the tap off. "I'm wet - what should I think about?"

"I need you to remember that you have two more days to pay the electric company," Javier said. "And that the electric lights are fine."

"Are you sure?" John Booth queried.

"Yes, sir, I found your bill on the refrigerator," Javier continued. "You have time to pay it, and you will remember. The electric lights have sufficient power."

All around, the soft yellow glow of the traditional bulbs and the cool white of the fluorescent lights began to glow. They could see the neighborhood lights through the window.

"Very good sir," Javier said. "Now sir, these new powers of yours - they are Booth powers – and they were meant for someone like you."

"Were they?" John murmured in wonder.

"They were," Javier intoned. "If you had not burned your powers out binding the Mater Vampire in your youth, you would have had similar powers all your life. Moreover, you would have been experienced in managing them."

"I would?" John was amazed.

"Of course you would sir," Javier continued. "And if these powers weren't meant for you - they would not have gone to you. Raven and Paul were also standing nearby - and they are both Booths."

"How do you know?" John asked.

"I don't know everything," Javier said. "But I can sense some things. You deserve these powers. You can manage these powers. Moreover, you will do good with these powers."

"I think you may be right," John said. "I do know one thing though - I need to change out of these wet clothes!" He hurried off into his bedroom.

"Thanks man," Paul turned to Javier. "That was a lucky escape."

"We had better be getting home," Javier said. "My parents worry about Jeroma, even when she is with me. Come along Bridget!"

"It's getting near our curfew too," Zarah and Benji Strahan admitted. "We need a lift home."

The Strahan siblings glanced expectantly between Javier and Fenton; while Paul Booth muttered apologetically that he did not yet have his full license. Whatever transport arrangements the youth had made earlier, had been disrupted by the power crisis.

"I will drop you off," Fenton Etheridge offered nobly.

The Tilton siblings, Javier and Jeroma had already left. Lena and Eduard exchanged glances, as thoughts of midnight make-outs were clearly running through their mind. Carlice and Fenton also turned towards their car, thinking perhaps they could squeeze in a kiss or two on the Favor's front porch, after taking the Strahan's home.

****

Carlice slept in as long as she could the next morning, but unfortunately, she knew that she would have to go to school. In the olden days, everyone would have gone to church on All Saint's Day and prayed for their deceased loved ones. While church could be boring at times, it was more relaxing than school, and Corpus Christi was a fun festival in some countries. Eventually, Carlice forced herself to get out of bed.

Sheriff Favor was busy in the kitchen, frying eggs for breakfast. "I thought you and I had better have something healthy to eat after last night," her mother announced.

Carlice tweaked the edges of her mother's little apron. "Don't let Damien see you wearing this," she said. "It might give him ideas."

"It's just to keep my uniform clean," the Sheriff huffed. "And Damien isn't looking for a cook - he doesn't really eat."

"Those weren't the ideas, I was referring to," Carlice retorted, but her mother remained obtuse. The Sheriff either did not know, or would not admit, the implications of a maid's costume.

There was a knock at the door, and Damien appeared. "Don't let Damien see what?" he inquired.

"Nothing," Carlice said, occupying herself with sipping her 'special smoothie', and poking her rare egg around on her plate.

"Did you solve the problem up by Carolina?" Sheriff Favor asked, partially because she wanted to know, and partially in order to distract him.

"Oh yes," Damien said. "In the end it was nothing. The good news is - I have got the treaty with South Carolina that I wanted!"

"You must tell me how you achieved that," the Sheriff ordered.

"I'll tell you what you need to know," Damien replied cryptically. "And I will eat one of those eggs if you don't mind, Sarah. There is goodness in an egg, even for a vampire, presuming you haven't overcooked it. Eggs are designed to sustain a growing chicken until it hatches."

"Coming right up," the Sheriff said. "One egg over-runny."

"I used to hate these," Carlice admitted, "And now they are the only sort I can have."

"Enjoy what you still can," Damien advised. The vampire was a bit smug and a bit avuncular, but Carlice had to admit, he was most often right.

Fenton's car purred into the drive-way, and Carlice washed down the rest of her egg with her smoothie. "Goodbye Mother, goodbye Damien, I must not make Fenton and Bridget late for school."

Carlice kissed her parent goodbye and trotted out into the street, where she climbed into the passenger seat of the Etheridge family car.

"Hey Fenton, Hey Bridget," Carlice exclaimed. "How are you both feeling this morning?"

"Good thanks, Carli," Fenton replied happily. "Did you have fun last night, aside from the drama at the Booth house?"

Bridget was on her mobile phone and was clearly talking to Javier Tilton. "You were wonderful last night," she gushed.

"You had better be talking about his mind magic," Fenton chortled sternly.

Bridget blushed. "Of course," she said. "But Javier really did save Mr. Booth from something nasty."

"I think so too," Carlice admitted. "Javier is handy to have around."

"And that is the way I intend to keep him," Bridget sounded smug and satisfied. She clearly was not experiencing the insecurities with her new boyfriend, that she had once experienced with Damien Nevermore.

"I hope I am useful too," Fenton said jovially, putting the car into gear and heading down the street towards the high school.

Carlice reached out to rest her hand on his knee: "I love you just the way you are," she murmured.

"I love you the way you are too," Fenton replied. "Even being a vampire comes in handy at times!"

"So what about children?" Carlice murmured.

"We will have lots of fun first, and then if children do not come naturally, we will foster some child that genuinely needs us," Fenton said.

"I think that you would make an excellent mother, Carlice," Bridget mused. "You would never be too old!"

"A mum like you would be rather cool," Fenton said. "Especially for a child who had a hard time elsewhere, because you would understand almost anything!"

"And in the meantime," Bridget suggested. "You can practice on Tiger. I am sure that he will warm to you very soon."

"I would like that," Carlice said. Visions of the cute ginger kitten curled up on her lap and purring began to form in her head. "Let me know when I can come over again."

ABOUT THE AUTHOR

Cecelia is an Australian author and poet who has a special interest in American Literature. In 1993 she completed a Master's thesis on H.P. Lovecraft and the 'Gothic' or 'weird tale'. She followed this with a study of the Fairy Tale Motif in Victorian Literature in 1996, also at Masters' level.

Today, Cecelia is hard at work creating her own fairy tales and myths.

Cecelia is also the author of:

Special Pictures to Talk About (ISBN: 978-0-646-97235-0), which developed out of her work on language delay and speech development in Kindergartens.
Silver Springtime (ISBN-13: 978-0-6481160-1-1), the first of a series of period romances following the developmental struggles of a group of teenagers attending a Christian university in the 1980s.
All for Love (ISBN: 978-0-6481160-2-8), the first of a reality television spin-off romance series.
Mystic Evermore (ISBN: 978-0-6481160-0-4), the first of the vampire series "Nevermore Parables".
Saints and Sinners (ISBN: 978-0-6481160-4-2), the second of the vampire series "Nevermore Parables".
Faith and Love (ISBN: 978-0-6481160-3-5) – the second "Silver Springs University" Christian college romance story.